While You Were Skiing

While You Were Skiing

MEGAN BYRD

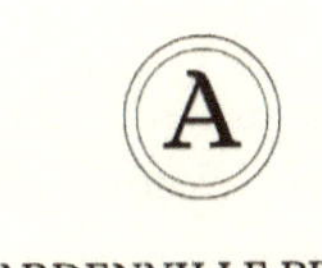

ARDENVILLE PRESS

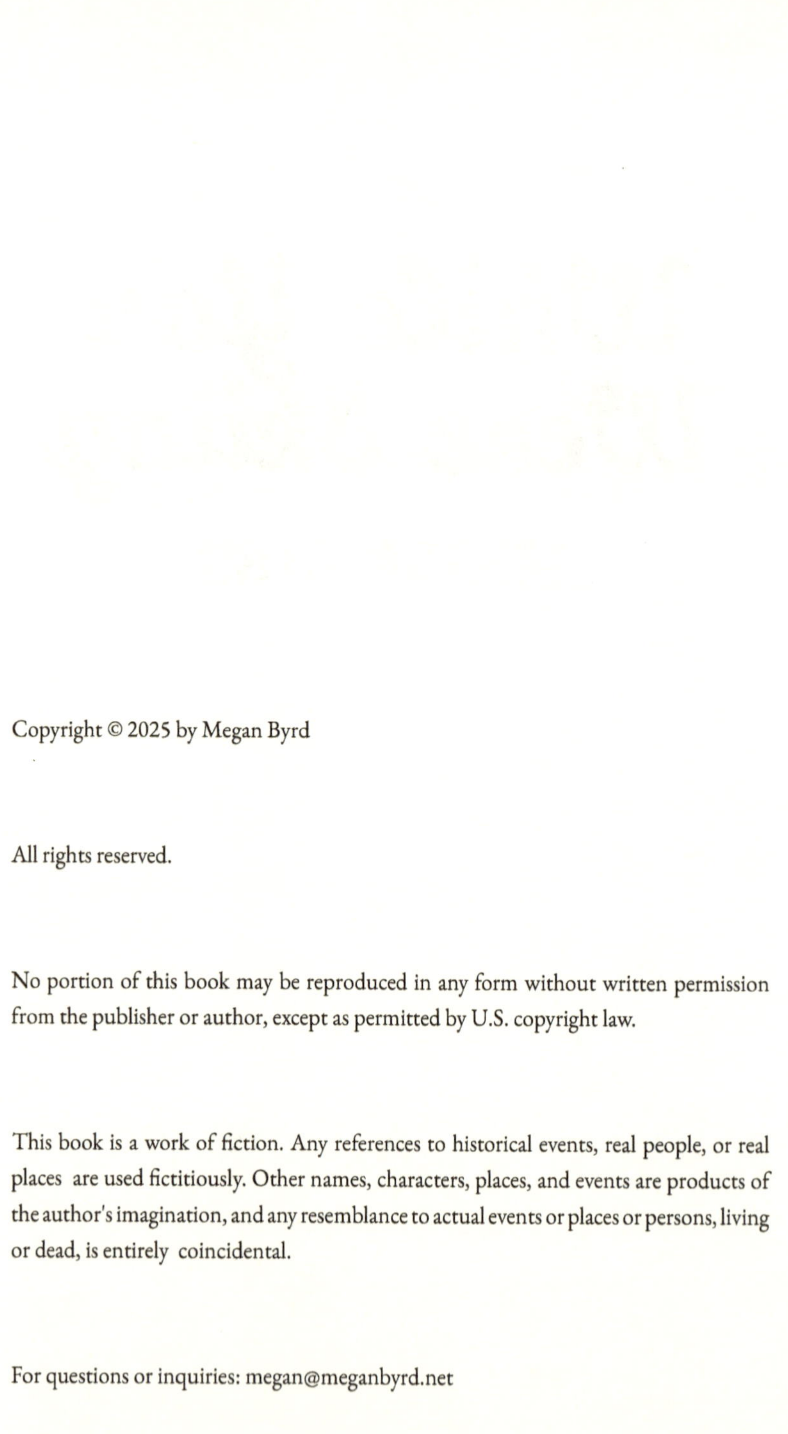

For Bettye, Lois, Louise, Maureen, Nancy, Susanne
and all the other amazing Grandmothers and Nanas

Chapter One

Piper

If someone had told me that running out of coffee creamer on a Tuesday in December would change my life, I'd have looked at them like they were nuts.

I'm in the break room, filling my favorite mug with coffee, being sure to leave some room for the hazelnut creamer I love so much. When I grab the container from the fridge, it feels lighter than it should be. My eyes narrow, wondering who's been pilfering it. I bet it's Terrance in accounting. He seems shifty. Hopefully, there's at least enough for this morning. I flip the cap and start pouring.

Movement out of the corner of my eye makes my head snap up. I freeze, my eyes stuck on the gorgeous face of the man who just walked in. My brain is whirling, wondering what Lucas is doing in the break room at—my eyes dart to the clock—seven fifty a.m. He's usually sequestered in his office by this time. Not that I'm complaining, because I welcome every opportunity to be in his presence.

His eyes meet mine, and I quickly glance away, worried he might have realized I've been staring.

"Uh, Paige?"

My brow furrows. Who's Paige? I look back at Lucas and realize he's talking to me, the corner of his mouth tipped up in amusement. He tips his head toward the counter.

"I think you may have overfilled your mug."

I glance down, my stomach dropping when I see creamer streaming down the sides of the cup. Setting down the now empty container, I dash over to the sink and grab a handful of paper towels to stop the beige river headed toward the edge of the counter. I mop it up, keeping my back to Lucas, mortified. There's a clink of the coffeepot spout against the edge of a cup, then the jostling of the pot back into its place.

Lucas picks up the container next to me and shakes it. My eyes remain trained on the soppy paper towels next to my mug, my cheeks burning with embarrassment.

"Bummer," he says. "Will you order more creamer, Paige?"

Indignation rises inside at the realization that he's the one who's been stealing my creamer and doesn't even know my name. I whirl around.

"First of all, my name is *Piper*, which you should know, *Lucas*, because we've worked together on several projects. Second, this is my personal creamer you've been using. Third, ordering creamer is not my job. Just because you're the top salesperson in the company doesn't give you the right to treat everyone else as if they're beneath you. I helped you win some of your big contracts, or was I just a faceless minion you handed a crystal bowl to after landing the Waterford account?"

He raises his hands in front of him, eyes wide like a deer in headlights. "Whoa, there. I wasn't trying to be rude. I'm sorry if it came off like that." His eyebrows knit together. "Is everything okay, Pai—I mean, Piper?"

A wave of horror hits me. I just yelled at Lucas Cahill, dreamy sales god. I've never been very confrontational. I usually just let things slide and hope people will change. Which of course, never works.

Lucas is looking at me like I've got two heads. I doubt he gets yelled at very often. Not with as smooth and handsome as he is. His ability to make connections with others is one reason he's so successful in the sales department.

I sigh, embarrassment overshadowing all other emotions. "I'm fine. I just don't like people taking things without asking." I feel sheepish for getting so worked up over a little creamer. But if I'm honest, it's not really about the creamer. It's more about the time of the year. The anger momentarily eclipsed the undercurrent of sadness, which was kind of nice.

"Well, I didn't realize it was yours. You should put your name on it or something."

I pick up the empty container and point to the initials written in Sharpie on the lid. "I did."

He makes a face. "My bad." He reaches into the fridge and grabs another bottle of creamer.

"That belongs to Christy," I say.

He inspects the bottle. "I don't see a name."

"Did *you* put any creamer in the refrigerator?"

"No."

I give him a pointed look.

He puts the bottle back. "Guess I'm drinking it black today." He gives me a nod and heads back to his office.

I slump against the counter. Did I really just cop an attitude with my office crush? I eye my full mug. Must be the lack of caffeine in my veins. I can be a little grumpy in the morning, which would surprise everyone in the office because I'm usually a ray of sunshine. Guess the season is hitting me hard this year. It's the five-year mark of the worst event of my life. I take a sip so it doesn't spill, then pick up the mug, wipe the sides, and toss the paper towels in the trash with the empty creamer bottle. My heart is beating fast from the encounter. Well, I finally got Lucas to notice me. Too bad he'll probably avoid me like the plague from now on. He definitely won't want to date me. Not that he'd ever be interested. Not with someone like me.

I still remember the first day I saw him. I'd been working for Elite Creative for two years in the graphic design department and he walked into our cubicle space and asked if anyone could help him put together a presentation for a client. I was too busy staring at his perfectly proportioned face with a long straight nose, teal green eyes, and wavy black hair to respond, but a guy in the department offered his assistance and the brilliant smile Lucas sent his way had me wishing I'd raised my hand.

We've worked in the same building for three years, and I've helped with a few of his sales projects, but Lucas obviously hasn't noticed me, as evidenced by the fact that he doesn't know my name. At least, he didn't until I verbally assaulted him. I shake my head, ashamed of my behavior.

Back at my desk, I shoot a Teams message to Christy in legal. We started at the company within a week of each other, but didn't meet until I stopped by her desk to ask about whether I could use a competitor's logo in an advertisement for one of our clients. When I saw the photo of an orange tabby cat on her desk, I knew we had to be friends. Now, we have lunch together most weekdays.

Piper: Can I be reported to HR for dressing down the co-worker who's been stealing my creamer?

Christy: Ooh, I can't wait to hear this story. I think they're more in the wrong than you, so I wouldn't sweat it.

Piper: Oh, I'm still sweating it. You won't believe who it was… *big eyes emoji*

Christy: Terrance?

Piper: That's who I suspected too, but no.

Christy: Gah! I need to know but I've got meetings until 11:30. Lunch at Marco's at 11:45? *salad emoji*

Piper: *thumbs up emoji*

Christy sits down across from me at the little bistro table I snagged in the corner of the restaurant.

"I ordered your usual."

She smiles at me. "Okay, spill."

I take a sip of my water before recounting the break room fiasco.

"No way!" she says. "*Lucas* is the thief? I never would have guessed."

"Me neither. Doesn't he have a Keurig in his office? Why even bother visiting the communal kitchen?"

She smirks. "Obviously, to steal the creamer. His sweet tooth must be as strong as yours." Her eyes light up. "Looks like you two have something in common."

"Too bad I blew any chance of getting on his good side by yelling at him."

Christy shrugs. "Who knows? Maybe he likes women he can't push around. I mean, at least now he knows your name."

I groan. "That was not how I imagined catching his attention."

"Well, whatever. Would you really want to date someone who doesn't show remorse about stealing other people's food items?"

"If he looks like Lucas, yes."

She chuckles. "I suppose I can't blame you. He is cute and wears the mess out of a suit. But I don't know if he's 'spill all your creamer' hot."

I roll my eyes. "Says the woman who *accidentally* set her trash can on fire to get a date with a jacked firefighter. Remind me again how that turned out?"

She purses her lips, but it doesn't hide her amused expression. "Okay, fine. Attraction makes people do odd things. In your case, it was a dressing down of your office crush."

I drop my head into my hands. "I'm never going to hear the end of this, am I?"

"Not unless it somehow ends up snagging you a date with the Luscious Lucas."

I scrunch up my face. "Ew, I don't like that description."

"Luminous? Legendary? Ooh, Lustful."

I put up a hand. "Just stop."

Thankfully, our server arrives and distracts Christy from her alliterative attempts to nickname Lucas.

"So, what are your Christmas plans?" I ask as we're walking back up the street to our office building.

"Brooks and I are driving up to his parents' house, and then we'll visit my folks on our way back here for the New Year's Eve party. You're coming to that, right?"

"Where there's free food and drinks? You know it."

She grins. "What about you? Going to get out of town this year?"

I have no plans whatsoever. Just like last year. Still, I don't want to sound as pathetic as I feel. "Nothing definitive, but maybe I'll check out the Botanic Gardens Blossoms of Light or finally take the train through Royal Gorge."

Christy's eyes light up. "Ooh, Brooks and I did that a couple of years ago. It was breathtaking."

We ride the elevator up to the sixth floor, where I get off, waving to Christy before the doors close to carry her up to the eighth floor. I glance over toward Lucas's office, but the light's off and the door's closed. He must be having a customer lunch, playing golf, or doing some other sort of schmoozing. Well, I hope he's done for the day. I'd rather put some more time and space between this morning's incident and seeing Lucas in the office again. Though, I doubt it's even a thought in his mind with as little as I seem to factor into his world. I, however, am going to be dwelling on it indefinitely.

As soon as the key touches the lock on my front door, the meowing starts from inside. You'd think I never feed Maui with as pitiful as she sounds sitting next to her empty bowl. I pick her up and cuddle her to me, enjoying the rumble of her chest when she begins to purr.

"Hello, sweet girl. Did you miss me?"

She rubs her head against my cheek.

I set her back down, then grab a can of cat food from the pantry. I scoop it into the bowl. Despite my attempt to block her from the food until I'm finished, she darts around my hand, winding up with gravy on her ear. I chuckle and scratch her back before grabbing a washcloth to wipe her off. She continues to wolf down her food, not fazed a bit.

After leftovers for dinner, I drag my Christmas tree out of the spare bedroom closet and set it up next to the fireplace. Even after fluffing the branches, it still looks a little sad. Maybe lights will help. I pull up some instrumental Christmas music on my phone and get to work. Only two of my four strands of lights work, but it's enough for my skinny six-foot artificial tree. Next comes a thick white ribbon swirled from top to bottom, which hides some of the tree gaps. All is going well until I open up the box of ornaments. Sitting on top is an artist's easel with a photo of me and my dad. I'd completely forgotten about it. Dad had given it to me our last Christmas together. I'd carefully stored it when we took down the decorations before I headed back to London to start my fancy new life as a working artist. Except none of that actually happened.

For the first three years after the accident, Christmas was on my naughty list. The season and all the painful feelings now wrapped up in it were still too fresh, so I put my head down and slogged through the month of December. Last year, while I still couldn't bear to drag out the tree, Christy cajoled me into attending the company's New Year's Eve party, which turned out to be fun. This year, I've been psyching myself up to decorate the tree. It was going fairly well until now.

I pick up the ornament, then sit down heavily on the couch, clasping the photo to my chest. I close my eyes in an attempt to staunch the tears. Maui jumps up next to me, then curls into a ball on my lap. I rub her head while my mind wanders miles away to Christmases long ago.

When my emotions have settled, I gently lift Maui off and set her on the cushion next to me. She stretches, then jumps down and wanders away. I stand up, placing the ornament on the tree at eye level. I outline it with my finger, then kiss my fingers and press them to Dad's face.

"Miss you, Dad," I whisper.

Over the next hour as I add the rest of the ornaments to the tree, a few knock the breath out of me with their memories, but I mostly hold it together.

At the bottom of the box is the tree topper. I set the angel on the top branch and plug it into the lights so the candle glows. Releasing a deep breath, I study the tree for a moment before opening up another box containing garland and caroler figurines for the mantel. Underneath them is a fluffy snowman with a red beret and matching scarf that always makes me smile. I carry him into the bedroom and set him on my dresser so I can see him from the bed.

Feeling exhausted from the trek down memory lane, I unplug the tree, put away the boxes, and head to bed, hopeful that tomorrow will be less emotionally volatile.

Chapter Two

Piper

When I get to work the next day, the last thing I expect to see is Lucas standing in the kitchen holding an industrial-sized bottle of hazelnut creamer. It makes the one in my hand look like a single-serve. He pushes away from the counter and holds it out to me, a sheepish smile on his face.

"Good morning, Piper. I apologize for stealing your creamer yesterday. And many days before that. Think this'll even things up?"

I'm stunned. Lucas seems like a completely different person. Where's the bravado and entitlement I saw yesterday?

I reach out and take it, feeling awkward double-fisting coffee creamer.

"Uh, thanks. I've never seen a creamer this size before."

He smiles, and my heart skips a beat. I've seen it many times at work, but this is the first time it's been directed solely at me. Does this mean my rant didn't put him off yesterday?

"It's from Costco."

My brow furrows. I don't picture Lucas needing to purchase items in bulk. Though maybe if he hosts parties for clients and needs a boatload of hors d'oeuvres?

"Ah." *So eloquent, Piper.*

Feeling like this interaction has reached its natural conclusion, I maneuver around Lucas to the fridge. I shove my regular-sized bottle under my arm so I can open the fridge and deposit both bottles inside. However, the entire fridge door is filled with bottles of hazelnut creamer. Confused, I turn and look at Lucas. He smirks and lifts a shoulder.

"So I don't have to drink black coffee for a while."

"That's one way to solve the problem." I shake my head and stick my bottles on a shelf, laying the extra-large one on its side so it'll fit.

When I turn, Lucas is still looking at me, his arms crossed over his chest. He certainly wears a suit well. Not wanting to be caught staring at him again, I turn my gaze to the clock on the wall behind him; the time reminds me there are things to do.

"I've got to get to a meeting. Thanks for the creamer."

I've just passed by him on my way to the door when he speaks.

"Actually, Piper? I was wondering if you'd have lunch with me today."

I freeze, my brain struggling to process his words. Lunch? Like a date? Surely not. I turn and assess his body language. He doesn't look nervous. Perhaps he's accustomed to people saying yes to his requests.

"Why?"

His eyes widen slightly, like I've caught him off guard. Maybe I'm right about Lucas always getting what he wants.

"I want to ask you something, but it requires a bit of explanation."

What could he possibly have to say to me?

"Please?" he adds, his expression sincere if not a little vulnerable.

My heart swoops. I'm more than a little curious. And that "please" made my insides swoon. What harm could it do?

"Okay. Marco's at noon?"

His shoulders drop, and an amiable smile replaces the straight line of his mouth from moments earlier. "How about Guard and Grace? My treat."

It's the swanky steakhouse just up the street I've yet to set foot in. Why not?

"Sure."

"Excellent. See you later, Piper."

He turns and exits, leaving me standing alone in the kitchen. I blink a few times, spotting the clock again and remembering my meeting. I quickly pour a cup of coffee and open one of the myriad hazelnut creamers in the fridge, shaking my head. Who does something like that? Someone who really wants to get on my good side. But why?

Piper: Can't meet for lunch today. Eating at Guard and Grace. *blushing emoji*

Christy: G&G?! Who with? Is this a date?! *fire emoji*

Piper: Lucas, believe it or not. And I don't know…? He says he wants to ask me something. *scared face emoji*

Christy: LUCAS!!! Go, enjoy. Meet me at Marco's after work for a debrief?

Piper: Deal. Wish me luck. *four-leaf clover emoji*

Christy: *horseshoe emoji* *fingers crossed emoji* *martini emoji*

When I enter the restaurant and look around, Lucas is seated in a booth near the back. He waves his hand, and I raise mine in acknowledgment before making my way over to him. A server appears and offers to hang up my coat. I hand it to him before sliding into the booth opposite Lucas.

"Want something to drink?" Lucas asks.

"Just water, thanks."

When the server returns with our drinks, he hands us menus. I'm thankful it hides my face because my eyes practically bug out of my head at the prices. *This* is why I haven't eaten here before. I scan the menu, looking for something relatively affordable before settling on the pasta. When the server returns, Lucas orders a steak, baked potato, and salad—all of which are a la carte—while I stick with the tortellini.

"So," Lucas says, "you're probably wondering what this is about."

I'm grateful he's jumping right in because, honestly, it's been a struggle to concentrate all morning wondering what he wants to ask me.

"There's really no delicate way to do this, so I'm just going to come out and ask. Would you come to my family's Christmas with me?"

Um, what?

"I'm sorry, I don't think I heard you right."

"I'd like you to join me for the Christmas holiday with my family. As my girlfriend."

I can't do anything but blink because my brain has short-circuited. Am I having an extremely lucid dream right now? Is this some kind of out-of-body experience where all my fantasies are revealed?

"Piper?"

I shake my head, trying to get things working again. While this sounds like a dream come true—my longtime crush asking me out—this feels sudden and not quite right. "I think there must be something wrong with my ears. I could have sworn you just asked me to be your girlfriend, when yesterday you didn't even know my name."

He frowns, running his hand through his hair, then leans forward, setting his forearms on the table. "Your hearing is just fine. I'm going to be completely straight with you. I was dating someone, but she broke up with me. However, I've already told my family I'm bringing my girlfriend, and my brother will tease me mercilessly if I show up alone. I really don't want to give him that satisfaction. He already wins at everything. I can't let him be right about my inability to hold on to a relationship too."

My heart tugs in sympathy. Now that I'm looking at him, there is a hint of sadness in his normally gregarious personality. It would be pretty hard to be hurting from a breakup and then be ragged on by family.

"I'm sorry about your breakup, but why ask someone you don't even know? Surely you have friends who could play this part or help you find someone who will."

He frowns. "I've asked around, but they all have plans because it's Christmas. Word around the office is that you're staying local, so I thought maybe you'd be game for an all-expenses paid holiday at a ski resort."

I sit back, surprised. He asked around the office? And who told him I didn't have holiday plans? Does everyone at work think I'm some sad, lonely spinster? Does *Lucas* think that?! It's not far from the truth, but still. It really doesn't paint me in the best light.

"Who told you I don't have plans?"

He waves my question away. "I know it's a lot to ask, but you'd really be doing me a solid here. I'll book you a day at the spa, give you a shopping spree in town, whatever you want. Just please, please say yes."

The thought of Lucas owing me does sound intriguing. But what exactly would I be doing? This is a *family* trip, after all. Will I be lying to a bunch of people? The thought twinges my conscience.

"I need more details. What exactly would saying 'yes' entail? How many days is this trip? What are my obligations?"

He nods. "Yes, good point. The trip is from the twenty-third to the thirtieth. We have friendly holiday-themed game nights, hang out, eat a lot of good food, and watch Christmas movies. Normal family stuff. You also have to pretend to like me. Maybe act like we're falling in love or whatever."

My eyes are as big as saucers. We'd leave in two days? Of course, it makes sense since the company closes for the holidays. I obviously wouldn't have to pretend to like him. I've got three years of practice with that one. And hanging out at a resort sounds pretty nice. So does being with other people, even if they are strangers. But his answers only bring up more questions.

"Where is this resort? And if we're acting like we're falling in love, does that mean we have to be affectionate? You know, like hold hands and kiss?" That alone might be enough to get me to agree. Kissing my crush doesn't sound like a bad time at all.

"We'd be staying in Steamboat Springs, which has a ski resort, but you can also go snowshoeing and hiking, and there are plenty of other activities. I suppose a little affection would help sell it, especially if we've been dating for about six months. We can play it by ear."

"Wait a minute. Why six months?"

"That's how long Laney and I were together."

Lucas and Laney. Very cutesy. "Wouldn't your family realize I'm not the same woman?"

He scratches his arm, avoiding my gaze. "No one met her, and I haven't really shared any details about us, so I think we're in the clear."

"Except if we've been together a long time, won't it be strange that I don't know anything about you other than where you work?"

This question seems to catch him off guard. Before he can respond, the server sets down our food. The pasta dish looks incredible. My stomach rumbles, and I want to dive right in, but don't want to appear rude. Thankfully, Lucas motions for me to eat. My first bite is heavenly. I close my eyes to savor the deliciousness. The pasta is super cheesy and the tomato sauce is very flavorful—definitely made in-house. Lucas's steak looks divine as well. I'd love to try a bite, but that's not something you ask on a first date. Not that this is an actual date. More like a business meeting.

"That's a good point. Email me a list of basic information about yourself," Lucas says," and I'll reply with mine."

I hold up a hand. "Wait a sec. I haven't said yes. You're asking me to give up my entire holiday to spend it with a bunch of strangers, telling lies the whole time? That doesn't exactly sound like a relaxing vacation."

He sighs. "You're right." He looks up at me with puppy-dog eyes and an earnest expression. "But Piper, I'm desperate. I'd be eternally grateful if you'd help me out. I'll even pay you."

I wrinkle my nose, turned off by the idea of monetary compensation. It kind of sounds like an adventure, and I do like novel experiences. I haven't acted since I attended musical theater camp in high school. This might actually be a little fun. Still, it's a big commitment. I definitely need to think it over. Maybe consult with someone who can give me an unbiased opinion.

"You're asking a lot of me, Lucas. I need some time to think about it."

"We don't have much time. If you can't do it, I don't know who else to ask."

The desperation in his eyes squeezes my insides. "I can give you a decision in the morning. Does that work?"

"Yeah, okay."

"And in the meantime, send me what you'd write on a dating profile."

He straightens up, hope returning to his eyes. "Of course. Let's exchange phone numbers too. Just in case. No pressure."

I huff out a laugh. No pressure indeed.

"Why wouldn't you do it?"

Christy looks at me like I might have a screw loose. Probably because she's listened to me wax poetic about Lucas for years.

"Because it's a crazy proposition. He wants me to stand in for some other woman and pretend we've been happily together for half a year!"

"And you hate the idea of spending time with your crush in possibly intimate and romantic situations where you might have to cuddle and kiss because...?"

When she puts it like that, it seems insane I'd even ponder turning Lucas down.

"But it's not *real*, Christy."

"Who says it couldn't turn into something real? Maybe when he gets to know you over the holiday and sees you with his family, it'll show him how awesome you are and how well you fit into his life. Besides, it's Christmas. Magical and romantic things happen this time of year."

I pause, not having considered the fact that it really *is* a chance to get to know Lucas for real. And maybe what Christy says could happen. Is this my chance to show Lucas I'm the woman of his dreams?

"But what happens when his family finds out we lied to them?"

"If you two fall in love for real, what does it matter?"

I don't have an argument for that.

"Look," she says, placing a hand on my arm, "I know this isn't exactly how things usually go, but think of it like having your relationship thrown into the deep end of the dating pool. After it's over, you'll know whether the two of you make a good fit. Then you won't have to spend any more years spilling coffee creamer on yourself whenever you get a glance at Lucas."

"That was *one* time," I retort.

Christy chuckles. "Honestly, Piper, what do you have to lose?"

I sigh because she's right. I have been drooling over Lucas for years. Why not find out if we have a real shot as a couple? And anyway, there's nothing keeping me from going. Well, almost nothing.

"Who's going to feed Maui if I go?"

"That's what pet sitters are for. And I know a great one. She's taking care of Bodie while we're gone. I'll give you her number."

"I guess I'm going to Steamboat Springs then."

"Cheers to that!"

Christy lifts her glass, and I clink mine to hers before taking a sip of my mixed berry martini. What have I gotten myself into?

Piper: I'll do it.

Lucas: Awesome. Thanks so much, Piper. You're a lifesaver!

Piper: I'm emailing you my "about me" info. Send yours back ASAP.

Lucas: Will do.

Lucas: Do you have your own ski equipment or will you need to rent some?

Piper: I'll need to rent it.

Lucas: No problem. Send me your boot and ski sizes and I'll have them reserved for you.

Piper: *thumbs up emoji*

Chapter Three

Piper

I'm picked up in a black car Lucas insisted he send for me. When I arrive at the airport, I'm glad he did because the car stops at a building I've never seen before. It's not the main terminal I'm used to flying out of. The driver unloads my bags from the trunk and leads me inside to a lounge area where, thankfully, I find Lucas already seated. He's furiously typing on his phone when I reach him.

"What is this place?"

Lucas looks up, a grin on his face. "This is the lounge for private transportation. Now that you're here, I'll tell the captain, and we should be ready to go in just a few minutes."

"I don't see where we go through security."

"The perks of private jets. If you're hungry, there's food over there." He nods at the two suitcases at my side. "Is that all your luggage?"

"Two bags are the limit, right?"

He shakes his head. "There are no limits when you have your own jet, Piper."

My mouth drops open. Your own what? "Tell me you're joking."

He shrugs. "Technically, it's the family plane."

I frown. Does Lucas come from money? "Is your family rich?"

"I mean, we're not hurting, but no one's retired and living on islands. We all have jobs."

I won't ask any more questions because I'd feel awkward, but I'm going to be on my guard, mentally preparing myself to meet people who might be slightly out of touch with reality. It suddenly makes sense why Lucas thought the company stocked the fridge with creamer.

"Hey, can we talk a little about this trip?"

"I thought we covered everything over email."

We've been trading messages ever since I agreed to participate in this scheme. I know how he takes his coffee—a generous helping of creamer, just like me—and that he was a Junior Olympic skier in his teens. He isn't a pet person and loves his job. He thinks being able to talk another person into his point of view is fun, and he's obviously quite good at it judging by the two sales awards he's won since he joined the company. And the fact that I somehow agreed to his insane proposition.

I know he has a sister just out of college who will be at the house and an older brother who's supposed to be there, but may not make it before Christmas. His parents, uncle, and grandmother are already at the place we're staying. There will be a family activity every evening, but plenty of free time during the day to do whatever we want.

I'm excited about the prospect of some alone time with Lucas. I've scoured the web for cute coupley things we can do together to show him I'm a genuine contender for his next actual girlfriend. I heard there's a hot tub at the house, which sounds amazing and could be romantic, especially if snow starts drifting down around us. I can scoot over next to him, and we'll stare into each other's eyes while flakes stick to our hair but melt on our hot skin. Love songs play over a speaker, and his eyes drop to my lips before he leans in and—

"Piper?"

I blink, realizing I'd drifted off there for a second. "What's that?"

"What did you want to talk about?"

"Oh, right. I just wondered how much physical affection your family is used to seeing from you and someone you're dating."

He coughs. "I've never brought a girlfriend to meet my family, so we can pretty much make it up. Seeing as we don't know each other and are going to continue to work at the same company after this, we probably should keep kissing to a minimum. But I think little touches and hand-holding would be okay."

My heart sinks. Does this mean he doesn't find me attractive? Did he really just ask me because he's desperate? "Whatever you want."

"Oh, I should warn you there's a chance we'll be sharing a room."

Internally, I'm freaking out. I didn't pack with that in mind. My pajamas are not the least bit attractive, just an oversized T-shirt and a pair of flannel bottoms. Nothing to be done now. Maybe I can win him over with my stellar personality and by nailing my role as his doting girlfriend. I'll have to stretch the minimal affection thing a little so he can see what dating me would truly be like. An occasional cheek kiss surely won't cross any boundaries we can't recover from.

"I can handle that."

"Great. Anything else?"

"Nope, I think that's it."

Lucas's phone dings in his hand.

"Perfect timing. We can load up and head out."

I follow Lucas out onto the tarmac, rolling my bags behind me. He doesn't seem to have any with him, but maybe they've already been loaded onto the plane. A crew member takes mine from me and ushers me up the stairs. When I step inside the small aircraft, a flight attendant offers me a bottle of water. I sit in one of the soft leather seats, and Lucas plops down in the chair across the aisle, his eyes glued to his phone. Can he use that on the flight?

"Can we keep our phones on?" I whisper across to Lucas, not wanting the attendant to overhear me.

"There's Wi-Fi, so just connect to it and you can send messages or whatever you want."

He returns his attention to his phone, and I pull mine out and text Christy.

Piper: We're taking a private jet!

Christy: Whaaaat?! Fancy. *starry-eyed emoji*

The attendant lets us know we're taking off, so I switch my phone to airplane mode and tap into the Wi-Fi. When I turn to Lucas, he's typing away on a laptop. I lean over far enough to peek at his screen. It appears he's working on a presentation.

"What's that?"

"Just something I'm fiddling with for a potential client. I can't quite get this to look right, though. I want it to have a futuristic feel, and it's just not working."

"Can I see your laptop for a sec?"

He shrugs and passes it over to me. I read the text he's got and grimace at the terrible clip art picture he's currently using. I switch fonts and grab some images from my favorite stock photo site. He doesn't have any of the programs I use for image manipulation, but I still create a slide that looks ten times better than his. I turn the screen back toward him.

"What do you think of this?"

His eyes widen. "That's amazing. How did you do that?"

I chuckle. "It's my job. I work in graphic design."

"You do?"

I sigh. He must not remember when I helped with his projects. "Did you not read my emails?"

He gives me a guilty look. "I glanced at them, but to be honest, my focus has been on wooing a new company. I told them I'd send over my proposal before Christmas, which means it needs to be done tonight."

"Why is this so important to you?"

He scowls and looks away. "Laney broke up with me because she said I focused too much on work and not enough on her. I was supposed to go with her to meet her folks at Thanksgiving but canceled to meet with this client."

I wince. "Yikes." Yeah, I wouldn't be too happy about that either. And the fact that he's working on a day we technically have off tells me a lot about Lucas's priorities. I'm sure the company is happy, but it doesn't look like he has much of a work-life balance. Maybe that's something I could help him with this week.

He sighs. "I know. I regret it now, but I can't put the rabbit back in the hat. I've put a lot of time into courting this client, and to lose them after I just lost someone I really liked is too much. If I can seal the deal, then I will scale back at work."

I can understand his need to prove that his loss is not completely in vain. I suppose I could do what I can to help him. It certainly wouldn't hurt my chances of getting him to see me in a positive light. If he achieves his goal, he'll be on top of the world. He'll want to celebrate with someone, and who better than the person who helped him succeed? It's a slight change to the game plan for winning Lucas's heart, but I can be flexible.

"What else can I do to help?"

His gaze returns to me, hope sparking in his eyes. "It doesn't bother you working on your day off?"

I shrug. "The sooner you get this wrapped up, the more fun we can have at the resort."

He smiles. "I like the sound of that."

We spend the rest of our flight passing the laptop back and forth until the proposal is complete. When we land and stand up, he gives me a hug, and I find I like the feel of his arms around me. Unfortunately, he lets go before I can really lean into the embrace. Oh, well. There's sure to be plenty more opportunities this week.

When we get off the plane, there's a car waiting. The driver loads our bags into the trunk while we settle into the warmth of the back seat. Lucas gives me a smile and a wink that make me feel like we're a team now. I smile back and then turn to look out the window at the mountains as we drive away from the airport. I could get used to this.

Chapter Four

Piper

The forty-minute car ride passes in silence. I watch the scenery while Lucas stares at his phone. Maybe Laney was on to something with him. Though I can understand being worked up over a big project. I'm sure he'll snap out of it once we get to the house. I wonder what it looks like. If they can afford a plane, is their house ginormous? It's got to sleep at least eight, so it can't be tiny. But we're probably staying in a rental since it's a holiday trip.

I'm a little nervous about the week ahead, especially since it appears I'm going to be skiing at least once. I had to visit a sporting goods store and find out my boot and ski sizes so I could text them to Lucas. While I was there, I grabbed a few pairs of wool socks, ski gloves, upgraded my winter coat to something waterproof, and bought a pair of insulated pants because odds are I'll be falling quite a bit when I first get started. While I haven't ever skied, I'm no stranger to winter sports, so it shouldn't be too hard to pick up. At least now I'll look cute doing it in my new threads.

The car stops on a street of almost identical rustic-looking houses bigger than anything I've ever lived in. The driver opens Lucas's door, and I exit the car behind him while the driver takes care of our luggage.

Lucas stares up at the house, a conflicted expression on his face. I grab his hand and give it a squeeze.

"You okay?"

He looks down at our joined hands, then up at me.

"Yeah. You ready for this? My family can be a bit much."

What does that mean? I plaster on a confident smile despite the butterflies in my stomach.

"Of course."

Lucas lets go of my hand and leads me through the open garage and into a mudroom filled with coats, hats, gloves, and other winter paraphernalia. I notice at least half a dozen pairs of skis lined up in the garage. All the Cahills must be skiers. We pass through another doorway into a hall that leads to the kitchen, which is filled with delicious smells.

"Hello?" Lucas calls. "We're here."

"Luc!"

A woman with shoulder-length blonde hair in a bob cut wraps him in a hug.

"So good to see you, hon." She lets go, then turns and eyes me up. "And who do we have here?"

"Mom," Lucas says, "this is Piper."

I stick out my hand. "Nice to meet you, Mrs. Cahill."

She bats my hand away and pulls me tightly against her, practically knocking the wind out of me. "Welcome, Piper. I'm Susanne, but everyone calls me Susie."

It's been so long since I've been hugged like this that I have to keep myself from melting into her embrace. "Thank you for letting me crash your family holiday."

"Nonsense," she says, releasing me. "We're so glad Luc has found someone special enough to share with us."

I cringe internally, but keep the smile stretched across my face.

"Did I hear someone come in?"

A man with salt-and-pepper hair comes in from another room. He looks almost exactly like Lucas.

"Hey, Dad," Lucas says, going in for a hug.

When Mr. Cahill spots me, he grins. "Who is this beautiful lady?"

"I'm Piper," I say.

"Luc's girlfriend," Susie says, giving me a wink.

I'm once again enfolded in arms that feel like home. Who knew a person could miss hugs so much?

"I'm Hank," Luc's dad says.

"Elise took the downstairs room," Susie says, "so you two are up in the bunk room."

"Thanks, Mom," Lucas says, then turns to me. "Follow me and we'll get situated."

My heart is pounding at the fact that we're definitely sharing a room. I wonder what size bed we have. Do I hope it's a full where we'll definitely have to touch, or would it be better for us to share a king while we get to know each other? Our suitcases are just inside the front door near the stairs, and Lucas grabs his bags before starting upstairs. I grab one of mine, knowing I'll have to come back for the other. I wonder if Lucas would be more chivalrous if I were his actual girlfriend. He certainly isn't acting like I think a boyfriend should. And does he prefer to be called Luc? He goes by Lucas at the office, so maybe it's just a family thing.

At the end of the upstairs hall, Lucas opens a door and motions for me to enter first. Perhaps he isn't completely devoid of manners. When I step inside, I'm surprised to see a set of bunk beds against the far wall. So much for cuddling. I drop my purse on the lower bunk and set my suitcase down.

"Actually," Lucas says. "Do you mind if I have that bed?"

"Are you afraid of heights?"

He shakes his head. "My brother and I used to share this room, and I'm used to sleeping on the bottom bed. I'm sorry."

I grab my purse and toss it up to the top bunk. "No, it's fine. It doesn't matter to me." I point to the large dresser next to him. "Are there specific drawers I should use for my clothes?"

He gives me a sheepish look. "The top three."

My eyes widen. I was joking, but apparently Lucas has preferences. Are there other things he's a stickler about?

"I noticed your parents call you Luc. Is that what I should call you?"

He shakes his head. "I prefer Lucas, but you can't help your nicknames, can you?"

You sure can't. A boy started calling me Pipsqueak in second grade, and it stuck until I graduated high school. It didn't matter that I shot up five inches at the end of middle school and was taller than the name-caller until he finally hit his own growth spurt in tenth grade.

"I'm going to grab my other bag and then unpack," I say.

"Let me get it for you," Lucas says, to my surprise.

Once we're unpacked, we head back downstairs and Lucas leads me to the family room where Hank is sitting on a couch with a man who could be his twin, an older woman with white curly hair, and a second woman who looks to be in her early twenties with blonde hair like Mrs. Cahill. Everyone is staring at us.

Lucas clears his throat, then lightly wraps an arm around my waist. "Piper, I'd like you to meet Uncle John, Grandma Nancy—but we all call her Nana, and my younger sister, Elise. Everyone, this is my girlfriend, Piper."

There's a cacophony of sounds as several people talk at once. "About time." "She's lovely." "Hold on to her, Luc."

"Nice to meet you all," I say with a smile and a small wave.

"Lunch is ready," Lucas's mom calls from the kitchen.

We assemble sandwiches and sit down at a dining room table big enough for twelve.

"So, Piper," Elise says, "what attracted you to my big brother?"

Thankfully, I've just taken a bite of my sandwich, so I take my time chewing while I work on an answer. Lucas and I didn't work out a "how we met" story or any kind of background about our relationship. Whoops. At least I can go with the truth for this question.

"It was his smile."

"He wore headgear for two years," Hank says.

Susie gently slaps his arm.

"What? It's true."

"What about you, Luc?" Nana says.

He looks up from his half-eaten sandwich. "What about me?"

"What attracted you to Piper?"

He glances over at me. "Our mutual love of hazelnut creamer."

I chuckle. We have an inside joke now.

"Hey," Susie says, "after lunch, will you two go into town and get stuff for dinner?"

"I'd love to," Lucas says, "but I have a work call I need to take in thirty minutes."

"But it's Christmas," she says, sounding disappointed.

"Piper and I can go," Elise says. She smiles at me encouragingly. "I can show her around downtown."

"Sounds good to me." I smile back even though I'm feeling a little nervous. This feels like the first test of whether or not I can pull this charade off.

Chapter Five

Piper

"That's our cute little bookstore, Off the Beaten Path, that also has a great little cafe," Elise says, pointing at a building through the windshield. "Some of their drinks are named after books and characters. My favorite is East of Eden, which is a dark chocolate lavender latte, but Mr. Darcy is also an excellent choice if you like cinnamon. And over there is Schmiggity's where they have live music and karaoke. If you're into line dancing, they have Two-Step Tuesday."

I follow her finger as she points out various businesses, enchanted by the adorable downtown area. The wooden-faced structures remind me of old Wild West movies. The snow-covered mountains jut up over the tops of the buildings. If it weren't for the paved roads and stoplights giving everything a modernized feel, I'd feel like I'd traveled back in time to a pioneer town in the 1800s. I'm amazed Elise is so familiar with the town. Her family must vacation here a lot. She pulls into a parking spot in front of Doc's Grocery, and we get out of the car.

Despite my resolve to support him, I'm a little disappointed Lucas has already ditched me for work. I know he's trying to win a big client, but surely he could have spared an hour for groceries. He seemed to miss the exasperated but resigned looks passed between his family at his announcement, which makes me think this has been a habit of his for a long time. But surely he'll get into the Christmas spirit once he's not so stressed about his current project.

I was a little overwhelmed meeting everyone at once. They seem nice enough, but it's been a long time since I've been around so many people socially. I kind of turned into a recluse after my dad died. Christy keeps trying to get me to come to her gatherings, but I've been hard-pressed to leave the comfort of my home in the evenings. Maui and I are currently working our way through a rewatch of *New Girl*, and it's been nice having a routine. Still, I realize I'm in a bit of a rut, so maybe all this time with strangers will help kick my life into a new gear.

Plus, those hugs were so warm and comforting. My dad gave the best bear hugs, and Hank's felt just as tight and inviting. Can a person go through withdrawal from a lack of physical touch? Regardless, I don't mind that Lucas's family is a bunch of huggers. I'll take all the affection I can get this week. Especially if Lucas is going to resist being a touchy-feely couple with me. The Cahills remind me a little of what my life used to be like, and I must say I do miss that warm familiarity between close relatives.

When we get inside the store, Elise suggests we split up the list to get through it quicker. It sounds good in theory, except this grocery store layout makes no sense. The canned goods are on the same aisle as the cereal, and bottled water and soda are right next to the produce. I'm going to have to visit each aisle in order to make sure I can find what I need. There aren't even any signs overhead to help me. I probably shouldn't expect a mom-and-pop store to be set up like all the chains I'm used to.

When Elise comes to find me, her cart filled with items, I've only found half of the things on my list.

"I'm sorry."

She waves me off. "Don't be. I know how wacky this store is. It took me years to memorize the layout. Why don't you get the lunch meat and cheese from the deli and I'll get the rest?"

I tear off my section and then hand Elise the rest of the list. There are a few people already at the deli counter when I arrive. I spot a ticket machine and grab a number. While I wait, I look at the confections on display in the adjacent bakery section. There are brownie bites decorated to look like reindeer, white-dipped Oreo snowman faces, and a log cake with powdered sugar dusted on top. I wonder if we need something festive at the house. I'll ask Elise when she comes back. I'm still staring at the table when I hear a voice behind me.

"I'd go with the snowmen. You can't go wrong with dipped Oreos."

I turn around and feel my cheeks heat when I see the man behind me. He has short brown hair, bright blue eyes, and a friendly smile, which makes a dimple pop in his cheek. He's tall enough that I have to tilt my head up to look at him properly. He's wearing a thick winter coat, but even so I can tell he's got muscles hiding underneath. I feel drawn to him but force myself to keep my feet planted in place.

"I don't know," I say. "Chocolate cake is pretty enticing."

He tilts his head from side to side, considering. "That's true, but you can have cake year-round. Snowmen Oreos are limited edition."

I grin. "Ooh, in that case, how can I not choose them?" I grab a container of Oreos and set it in the cart. "Are there any other limited-edition things I should get while I'm here?"

He smiles down at me. "*I'm* limited edition."

My eyes widen. I had an inkling he might be flirting with me, but he straight-up confirmed it with that comment. And while I'm definitely attracted to him, the whole reason I'm in this town is because I'm trying to get Lucas to fall for me. However, I suppose it can't hurt to have a little fun with this stranger. I'm probably a little rusty with my dating skills. My last serious relationship was while I was in college.

I raise an eyebrow and run my eyes over his body, enjoying this dance of words. "You certainly are. However, I don't think you'll fit in the cart."

He chuckles. "You're probably right."

"Number twelve," the deli counter clerk calls.

I hold up my slip of paper. "That's me," I say, disappointed that our banter is ending so soon.

I step over to the counter. "I need two pounds of turkey, one pound of roast beef, two pounds of ham, and two pounds of cheese, please."

"Which turkey?"

He waves at the glass. There's oven roasted, Cajun, honey, and smoked. The list just said turkey. "Oh, uh...what do you recommend?"

"Most people get the oven roasted."

"I'd choose the smoked," a voice says over my shoulder.

Goosebumps rise on my arms as I realize the flirty man is standing close behind me. The way he talks makes me think he's familiar with this store.

"I'll take the smoked."

"What type of ham?"

My eyes dart back to the case. Black Forest, Virginia, honey-roasted, capicola. What is capicola? Is there no regular ham? I turn to my left until I catch the cute guy's gaze. I raise both eyebrows, which I hope is enough of a signal that I want his help. He leans down, his cheek almost touching mine, and whispers into my ear. "Definitely the Black Forest ham. And I'd go with half provolone and half Havarti. They're both amazing on sandwiches."

I shiver from his warm breath skating over my skin. He's clean-shaven and smells fantastic. Part of me wonders what it'd feel like to have his cheek pressed against mine. But as soon as I have the thought, he pulls away and straightens up. I cough to clear my throat and my head.

"Black Forest ham, please."

When asked about the cheese, I parrot the man's words. When everything is sliced and in bags, I take it from the counter and turn to the man. "Thanks for your help. Are you local?"

"I used to be, but moved away after college. What about you? Just visiting?"

I nod. "I'm here for the holiday."

"If you want, I could show you around. I'm Mac, by the way."

He holds out his hand, and I slide mine into it, enjoying the warmth and how small my hand looks compared to his. "Piper."

We smile at each other, our hands still joined until a shout nearby makes us flinch and let go.

"Mac!"

He turns just in time to catch someone flying at him. I realize it's Elise when he spins her around and I see her face. She spots me and grins, then pats Mac's shoulder. He sets her down.

"I was wondering when you'd get here," Elise says. "Dad didn't think it'd be until tomorrow."

"I caught an earlier flight," Mac says.

"Well, welcome," she says. "And I see you've already met Piper."

He looks at me, his expression puzzled. "Is she one of your friends from school?"

She gently slaps his coat. "No, silly. Piper is Luc's girlfriend."

His eyebrows furrow. "What? I thought his girlfriend's name was Laney?"

Elise shrugs. "Nope. Piper, this is my oldest brother. His name is Matthew, but everyone calls him Mac. Please excuse his grumpy demeanor."

My stomach drops. I can't believe I was flirting with Lucas's brother. What's he going to think of me knowing I'm dating someone but flirting with another man? Ugh. I have to get it together. Maybe Mac will just interpret our banter as me being friendly. After all, I didn't say or do anything too incriminating. He was the one spouting off all the limited-edition stuff. I was just being polite and going along with it. Yeah, that's it. I almost believe myself.

I can't get distracted. Yes, Lucas's brother is attractive, but that doesn't have to mean anything to me. Lucas is also hot. I need to concentrate on my goal and keep my eyes on the prize of showing Lucas how good we could be together.

I glance over at Mac. His eyes dart to mine and then away again, a grim line where his smile used to be. It's the first I've seen of his so-called grumpy demeanor. Was he putting on a show for me earlier? Acting how he thought he should to catch my attention? It certainly worked, even though I shouldn't want to give him any of my consideration. If that was a fluke and he's actually a stick-in-the-mud, it'll certainly help me put my best effort forward with Lucas. Because that's why I'm here. For Lucas. I need to just forget about his handsome older brother.

Chapter Six

Mac

That was certainly an unforgettable way to make a first impression. Who flirts with their brother's girlfriend? Though to be fair, I didn't know Piper was dating Luc. All I saw was a beautiful woman standing in the bakery and I knew I had to get closer. Luc and I rarely have the same taste in women, so there was no way I'd ever consider her being the mysterious girlfriend I've heard so little about. I was really enjoying the fun, teasing conversation Piper and I were having before Elise crashed the party. Maybe I should be embarrassed that I told Piper I'm limited edition, but that was an epic in-the-moment line. I bet I could use that again with someone my brother isn't dating.

Is Piper going to tell Luc what I said to her? If so, oh well. Maybe he'll see it as a compliment that I think his girlfriend is attractive. Or he could be livid over the fact that I was hitting on someone he obviously cares a lot about. This is the first woman he's brought home to meet the family. If he's mad, I'll just explain that I wouldn't have flirted if I'd known who she was. Maybe it'll teach him to actually talk to his family about what's going on in his life. I was beginning to think he'd made up a girlfriend to get Mom off his back about how much he works.

My only real problem is figuring out how to spend a week together with a woman I brazenly flirted with seconds before learning a little wordplay is all that will ever pass between us. At least I should be able to avoid her for most of it. She'll be hanging out with Luc and I'll go skiing or hiking or do something else that gets me outdoors and away from the house. Maybe I can make it my mission to entertain Elise and stay far away from Piper. Besides, it was one harmless interaction. Surely she understands that. Had I known, I never would have done it. But who could have guessed Luc would fall for someone like Piper? She's petite with long black hair, and Luc usually goes for tall, leggy blondes. Though maybe that's his unserious type and he's finally found someone he really sees a future with. I mean, six months of dating is like an eternity for him. I'm impressed he's found someone who can tolerate him for that long.

I'm kidding, of course. He's my little brother, so it's required that I make fun of him. Plus, I don't think he's dated a woman longer than two months in the past couple of years. His focus has been on work, which hasn't seemed to leave room for anything else. In fact, I'm surprised he's even here. He skipped last Christmas for some big work thing. I think Mom guilted him about that enough that he actually showed up this year.

When I arrived at the house earlier, Mom put me in the room across from the one I used to share with Luc. Apparently, that's the couple's room this year, which is a little strange because it has two bunk beds in it. But my new room has a twin bed I barely fit on, while the bottom mattress of the bunk beds is a full, so I guess that makes sense.

On my way to drop my stuff off in my room, the door across the hall was closed, and I could hear Luc speaking with a raised voice. At first I was concerned he and his girlfriend were fighting, but Mom said he was working. All I could do was roll my eyes at that. When Luc was here for Christmas two years ago, all he did was work, according to Mom. Not sure if that was better or worse than not showing up at all last year. Maybe I'll sit him down and encourage him to let go of work this year to make Mom happy. Of course, I wasn't here the last two years either, but that's because I was overseas for work. Now that I'm back in the States, I asked for Christmas leave well in advance, like the responsible oldest son that I am.

After getting situated at the house, Mom told me Elise and Luc's girlfriend were doing the shopping, so I came to town to help. And that's how I ended up getting a little too friendly with Piper. At least I didn't kiss her cheek when I whispered in her ear. I was very tempted, especially after I got a whiff of her floral perfume. It drew me in like the Pied Piper. Ha. Piper. *That was bad, Mac.* At least I know we'll have dipped Oreos at the house. They're one of my favorite Christmas treats. Elise just shook her head when she saw them in Piper's cart and reminded me there are plenty of sweets at the house. That may be true, but I can't pass up an opportunity for white chocolate dipped Oreos.

While the women wait in the checkout line, I head next door to grab the wine and beer we'll need for the week. I don't know what Piper likes, so I text Elise. She tells me to just get the usual, which doesn't sit right with me. We should honor our guest. I text Luc, but he responds with a question mark. How does he not know what his girlfriend drinks? Surely he isn't that obtuse. Frustrated, I march back to the grocery store. The women are still waiting in line. My first glance at Piper makes my heart jump. Why does she have to be so pretty? And funny. And off limits.

I blow out a breath and make my way over to them.

"Done already?" Elise says.

"No, because you didn't answer my question." I turn to Piper. "Would you prefer wine or beer at the house?"

She scrunches up her nose, which I find adorable. *Stop it, Mac.*

"I'm not a huge drinker, but I do like Moscato. However, don't get something just for me."

"You're our guest."

Elise chuckles. "Typical Mac."

I frown at her. "What's that supposed to mean?"

"Nothing bad. You just like to take care of everyone."

"So?"

She blows out a breath. "You can't relax and go with the flow because you're too preoccupied with how everyone else is feeling. It's got to be exhausting."

Her words pull me up short. Is she right? Caring for others is how I show love. Is there such a thing as being too considerate?

"I fail to see how being kind is a bad thing?"

"It's not, but we don't need protecting. We're all adults. You're allowed to have fun and do things just for yourself. You don't always have to cater to the family's wishes."

Now it feels like she's alluding to things other than just making sure everyone has something to drink at dinner. My eyes drift over to Piper. I had momentarily forgotten she was here and witnessing our little back and forth. No need for her to get swept up in the Cahill family drama.

"Well, I'm going back across the street. I'll meet you back at the house?"

Elise rolls her eyes and motions for me to go.

I catch Piper's gaze again, and she gives me a questioning look. I shake my head, smile, then turn and get back to the mission, Elise's words running through my head all the way back to the house.

Chapter Seven

Piper

"So, Piper," Susie says while we're all seated at the dinner table, "Luc told me you met at work. How long have you been at Elite Creative?"

"Five years."

"What do you do there?" Elise asks.

"I'm a graphic designer. I help create the slides and illustrations for sales presentations, among other things." I look over at Lucas seated next to me and give him a wink, hoping it'll remind him about how I helped him on the plane ride over here. Unfortunately, his focus is on his lap where he's typing frantically on his phone. I frown, then nudge him with my elbow.

His head snaps up. "What's that?"

Susie sighs. "Do we need to implement a 'no phones at the dinner table' rule again this year?"

"Yes," Elise says, glaring at Lucas.

He shoves his phone into his pocket, then picks up his fork and spears a green bean. "Sorry. I'm just trying to win over a very big client."

"Surely it can wait until after the holiday, Luc," Susie says.

He frowns, but doesn't respond.

The table is quiet. It's quite obvious that his family is not happy about his work habits. Maybe I should focus on getting him to loosen up and have more fun while we're here together. I don't know what he likes to do for fun besides skiing, but perhaps I can quiz him when we're alone in our bedroom. We won't be doing anything in there besides sleeping, but I've wondered what kind of kisser he might be. Does he just dive right in or is he slow and patient, taking his time? If he kisses like he works, it's probably pretty intense. I'd really like to find out. Which means I need to be a lot more flirty. I know he said we should keep affection to a minimum, but if I'm playing to win, I need to use everything in my arsenal.

"Did you join Elite Creative straight out of college?" Elise asks, trying to diffuse the obvious tension in the room.

"I went to grad school, but joined the company soon after that."

"Does that mean you're about thirty then, dear?" Nana chimes in.

I smile at her sweet face. She's been pretty quiet throughout dinner, but now she's looking at me with keen interest. "Yes. I'm exactly thirty."

"Ooh, Luc is dating an older woman," Elise says, a teasing lilt to her voice.

"He needs someone to help him grow up," Uncle John says. "Maybe it'll help him set his priorities straight."

I frown. Does his family think he's irresponsible? Also, how old *is* he? Yet something else I need to find out. Somehow, our emails didn't include birthdays. I glance over in time to see his lips turn down slightly before his brilliant smile snaps firmly back in place.

"I think I'm doing just fine. However, Piper is great, and I'm lucky to have her."

He turns his smile on me, and my lips stretch wide in response. I know he's talking about me being his cover for the week, but I can't help pretending for a second that we're an actual couple and he sees how amazing we are together. I reach for his hand and squeeze it. I notice his eyes widen a bit in surprise and quickly let go.

"Mac, are you seeing anyone right now?"

"No, Nana," he says. "I'm too busy with work."

"Luc said you're a pilot. Which airline do you work for?" I ask, wondering if both brothers are workaholics.

He turns his attention to me, and it feels like his gaze pierces straight through me. "I fly for the Air Force."

That definitely explains the short haircut and stacked body. He's in a long-sleeve Henley, and that shirt is working extra hard to contain all those muscles. Not that I'm complaining, but I'm supposed to be ignoring him and focusing on Lucas, who's in shape but nowhere near as built as his brother. It's probably not great that I'm comparing the brothers' physiques. *Focus, Piper.*

"Wow. What types of planes do you fly?"

"F-16s."

"Is that a plane that carries people or one that carries supplies and tanks?"

Lucas chuckles, earning him a glare from Mac.

"No," Elise says. "Have you seen the movie *Top Gun*?"

My eyes widen. Mac flies fighter jets? "Whoa. Is it scary?"

Mac straightens in his chair as if he's coming to attention.

"No, it's an adrenaline rush. Dogfighting at five hundred knots is a high like no other. Flying is the most thrilling thing I've ever done."

It's amazing watching him come alive and light up from within as he talks about his job. It reminds me of how I used to feel when I painted. I'm enjoying this tiny glimpse of the man I first met. The sparkle in his eyes lasts until Nana's next question.

"What about your social life? Surely you can meet someone off-base."

All joy leaches out of his face. His brows furrow and lips turn down in a deep frown.

"It doesn't make sense if I'm just going to be moving here in a year or two."

Susie's face lights up. "I can't wait to have all my kids in the same state again. South Carolina is too far away, Mac."

He shrugs. "I have only so much control over where I get stationed. You two really should come visit while I'm still there. I can take you to the beach."

"You know we prefer the mountains," Hank says. "I can't get enough trout fishing."

"If you come, we can go deep-sea fishing. There are trout out there, plus grouper, mackerel, and even sharks."

Hank's eyes sparkle. "Sharks, huh? That might be fun." He looks at me across the table. "What about you, Piper? Do you like to fish?"

"I did some fishing with my dad when I was little, but not in years. He showed me how to clean and fillet what we caught and cook it over a campfire."

Mac's head swings over to me, surprise on his face. Guess he pictured me as an indoor, girly girl. Most people do, but there's more to me than meets the eye.

"Yuck," Lucas says. "Cleaning fish is disgusting."

Mac looks away, dropping his gaze back to his plate, pushing food around with his fork. There's no trace of the friendly, smiling guy from the grocery store or the exuberant man who obviously loves his job.

After we clean up, Susie pulls out plastic containers of sugar cookies, frosting, sprinkles, and a variety of candies.

"Tonight's family activity is the cookie decorating challenge. Make as many as you want, but you can only submit two for judging. John and Nana are the judges. Winner gets the crown and chooses tomorrow's activity."

I'm excited. I haven't decorated cookies in years, but anything involving design and color revs me up. I scoot over next to Lucas. "Is there really a crown?"

He smiles down at me. He's a few inches taller than I am, but nowhere close to his brother's height. "Yes. It's very tacky, but our family is quite competitive, as you'll see. Don't worry about it if you don't win. I was champ for two years, but Elise won the last two years because neither Mac nor I were here. We're all pretty skilled with some icing."

I feel my hackles rise. Lucas apparently has no faith in my skills. I'll just have to let my cookies do the talking. I certainly wouldn't mind taking the crown and seeing how he handles defeat. My guess is that it doesn't happen very often. I simply smile and shrug a shoulder, then turn and look around the table. There are sweater-shaped cookies, circles, stars, wreaths, and trees. I think I'll make one of each.

Lucas pulls out a chair for me and takes the one to my left. Elise sits down across from Lucas and motions with her fingers that she's got her eyes on him. Susie sits next to me, and Hank is across from her. Mac sits down directly across from me, his face blank. Actually, everyone seems to have their game faces on. I quickly tamp down my smile, realizing Lucas wasn't joking about his family. Okay then. Maybe I won't win, but at least I'll have fun decorating.

"Is it okay if I play some holiday music while we ice cookies?"

Susie smiles at me. "Wonderful idea. Elise, grab the speaker for Piper, please."

Elise gets up and races down the hall, back in a flash with a little black cylinder. "Here."

She sits back down, her body rigid. I've never felt this much tension over cookie decorating. I connect my phone and start a playlist of instrumental holiday classics.

"Ready..." Hank says. "And go!"

Hands fly across the table, grabbing cookies and icing. I sit back and watch the initial flurry, noting that everyone has hoarded cookies onto their decorating plates. I select a tree and look around for the green. Lucas has it.

"May I use the green after you, Lucas?"

His body is hunched over his cookie, blocking it from view. "Sure."

I survey the table while I wait. Everyone guards their plate like they're hiding secret plans. After five minutes, Lucas still has the green. "Are you going to be finished soon?"

He grunts, which really isn't an answer, so I decide to pivot away from a traditional tree. Pink icing sits untouched on the table, so I grab it and get to work. I use pearl-colored sugar balls and other accoutrements to make garland, lights, and ornaments. There aren't any sugar stars for the topper, so I create my own. When I'm finished, I carry it over to the cookie rack on the island. There are already a dozen other cookies there, and some look pretty good. I feel like I'm on a Food Network competition show, and it's pretty thrilling. Maybe I could have been a food decorator in another life.

When I return to my seat, I grab a sweater cookie and make the ugliest holiday monstrosity I can think of. It won't win the crown, but I'm having fun and that's what matters to me. I'm happily ensconced in a bubble of decorating, and time passes without me noticing. When I look up after finishing a circle cookie, the table is empty. I spot Mac and Elise in the living room with John and Nana watching *It's a Wonderful Life*. Lucas is nowhere to be seen, and Susie is wiping down the kitchen counters. There are still a few undecorated cookies on the table.

"How long have I been alone?" I ask Susie when I bring my finished cookie to the island.

She gives me a warm smile. "About thirty minutes. Are you finished?"

"Yes, unless you want me to ice the remaining cookies."

She shakes her head. "Nana likes to eat plain ones, so we'll leave them for her."

"Since I'm the last one, I'll clean up the table."

"First, pick your top two cookies for judging and add them to the lineup."

There are two rows of paper plates, each with a cookie in the center. I grab two plates and consider my options. I settle on the pink Christmas tree and the cookie I turned into a snow globe with a scene of an ice skater on a frozen pond. When I set them next to the others, Susie mixes the plates up a bit and then calls for Nana and John.

I clear off the kitchen table, rinsing icing bowls and wrangling rogue sprinkles with a brush and dustpan. Then, I wipe down the table with a cleaning rag. John and Nana make noises of surprise and delight while they consider the cookies. They banish me and Susie to the living room while they make their final selections. After a few minutes, we're all called back to the kitchen table, where there are three plates with napkins covering them.

"This year's competition was pretty stiff, but we've come to a consensus," John says, smiling at everyone.

"In third place," Nana says, taking the corner of one of the napkins, "we have..."

She whips the napkin away, revealing my pink tree. "The flamingo tree!"

I chuckle. "That's mine. I like the name, by the way."

Lucas puts an arm around my shoulders and gives me a squeeze. "Top three on your first try. I'm impressed."

I'm not sure whether he's being sincere or patronizing. I'll be generous with my interpretation, especially since he's also touching me of his own accord. It's definitely nice feeling like part of a duo.

"Second place," John says, "is...classic Christmas tree!"

It's a textured green tree with white icing added for snow and a little red bow at the top, like something you might see in a forest. It's very cool.

"Yesss!" Lucas says, releasing his hand from around me and thrusting it in the air.

"I like the textured icing," I say, holding up my hand for a high five.

He smacks it hard enough that my palm stings a little. "That must mean my wreath is the winner."

"Not so fast," Elise says, arms crossed. "My *Starry Night* star is pretty awesome."

I glance over at Mac, wondering if he'll chime in, but he's silent, his face still stony. Is he concerned about losing? I'm not a fan of sore losers. Maybe it's just his resting facial expression. No wonder he's known as a grump.

"This year's winner blew us both away with its intricacy and holiday spirit," Nana says. "First place goes to..."

John grins and yanks the napkin off the plate. "Snowy skater!"

Everyone stares down at the round cookie on the plate. My design won. I'm actually a bit shocked.

"That's amazing," Elise says, bending closer. "It looks like a real snow globe."

"Whose is this?" Lucas demands.

I raise my hand. "Mine."

He gapes at me. "How did you do that?"

I smile. "I *am* a graphic designer."

His face morphs into a scowl. "That's got to be cheating. You're a professional. I should win."

My expression opens into surprise. "What?"

"Now, now, Luc," Susie says. "It's all in good fun. You should be happy your girlfriend is so talented."

He rolls his eyes. "Whatever."

Yikes. I do *not* like this look on him.

"Give her the crown," Elise says, clasping her hands together.

Susie opens a cabinet and pulls out a sparkling crown with silver, green, and red gems on it. It is ridiculously gaudy and looks like something they'd give to the winner of a Miss Italy pageant. She places it on my head, and it falls over my eyes, balancing on my ears.

"It's a little big," I say, pushing it back so I can see.

Elise chuckles. "We had to find one big enough for Luc's huge noggin."

He narrows his eyes at her, still frowning. "Because I'm the one wearing it most often."

"But not this year!" Elise crows. "Girls rule!" She raises her hand to me, and I slap it.

Lucas stalks out of the kitchen and disappears up the stairs. Jealousy does not suit him at all.

"Congratulations," Nana says, coming over to shake my hand, which humors me. "You did an excellent job. It's almost too pretty to eat."

John pats me on the back. "Great job, kiddo. Way to beat the socks off Luc. He needs taking down a peg every once in a while. You're going to be very good for him."

It feels nice being welcomed and included like this. While Lucas has soured the evening a bit for me, I do enjoy being surrounded by others and having my accomplishments applauded. It's nice to have people in my corner again.

Everyone clears out of the kitchen, and I consider checking on Lucas, but Elise grabs my arm and steers me to the living room. "I'm so glad Luc has finally met his match. I think you're just what he needs."

"Thanks, I guess."

"Come play cards with me and Mac. Let Luc calm down a bit. Sometimes he needs a few minutes, but he'll be okay."

I hadn't considered that his intense nature, while great for excelling at business, might have some downsides. As long as he's able to sort himself out, I can deal. None of us are perfect after all. I've got my own weaknesses.

I sit down at a card table, and Elise explains the rules of a game I've never played. When I look up at Mac, he's gazing at me, a divot between his eyebrows.

"You deserved to win," he says. "Congrats."

"Thank you," I say, looking away before I get caught in his intense gaze.

After playing a few rounds of cards and losing all of them, I decide to call it a night. When I get up to my room, Lucas is typing on his phone. He looks over at me.

"Sorry about earlier. I can be a bit of a sore loser. It's something I'm trying to work on. Your cookie really was fantastic."

It's nice that he recognizes his shortcomings and can apologize. The anxiety I was feeling eases. "It's fine. I liked your designs. I see why you win so much."

He nods, then goes back to his phone.

"Hey, uh, when's your birthday and how old are you? I feel like we should have covered that."

"I turned twenty-five on June 29th. We should get to bed. We'll need lots of energy tomorrow."

My brow furrows. "What's tomorrow?"

"Skiing, of course."

He gives me a wide grin that I try to mirror while internally freaking out. We're skiing already? I thought I was going to have a few days to psych myself up for it. Oh well. I'm sure it'll be fine.

Piper: Guess who won the cookie decorating contest? *photo of Piper wearing a crown*

Christy: Nice headgear. Do you get to keep it?

Piper: Sadly, no. But maybe I'll wear it all week and enjoy being queen.

Christy: *laughing emoji* How's Operation Show Lucas How Awesome You Are going?

Piper: Wow, that's a mouthful. And Operation SLHAYA is not going great.

Piper: We should call it Show Lucas Awesome You so it can be Operation SLAY.

Christy: Yesssss! Love it. *dancing emoji*

Piper: Also, I accidentally flirted with Lucas's brother. *facepalm emoji*

Christy: You what?! *wide-eyes emoji*

Piper: In my defense, I didn't know who he was, and HE started it. But I promise I'll do better tomorrow. How's your vacation going?

Christy: Brooks and his brother didn't break any windows putting up the tree this year, so that's a win.

Piper: Hope there aren't any hospital visits either. *ambulance emoji*

Christy: *fingers crossed emoji*

Chapter Eight

Mac

It took me a long while to fall asleep last night. I think part of that had to do with the couple across the hall. I know I should be happy my little brother found someone he likes enough to introduce to the family. I thought he was dating a woman named Laney, but I could have heard that name from one of the guys on base. Some of them run through women like tissues. It's not my modus operandi, but I won't begrudge them their choices. Military life can be stressful, and anything that helps blow off steam is welcome. I prefer to reduce the pressure through paintball, fishing, and a recreational softball league.

I must admit, it was pretty entertaining watching Luc lose to his girlfriend in cookie decorating. He's always been intense about anything competitive. He got kicked off several sports teams for being too aggressive and arguing with coaches and referees alike. Of course, it's also why he did so well in skiing. He practiced moguls and courses until he had every bump and divot memorized. It's probably why he also does so well in sales. I'm pretty sure he studies his clients until he knows everything about them.

This trait has raised a red flag in my mind about him and Piper, though. Since they work in the same building, he knew she was a designer. Why was he so surprised at her decorating talent? Surely she's shown her artistic skills in other ways before. Was he just upset about losing, or does he actually not know her that well? If they've been together for six months, it seems like plenty of time to learn all about Piper. Maybe he hasn't been as observant as I think a boyfriend should be. Not that I'd be shocked if that's the case. He can be a little self-absorbed.

Truth be told, I was incredulous when that snow globe cookie was revealed. It looked just like a real ornament you'd find on a tree. I don't know how anyone is going to be able to eat such an amazing work of art. It's in the plastic tub with all the other cookies, but I'd wager it's still in there when we all go home unless Piper eats it herself. I spotted half a dozen other cookies that I think are also hers. She has a unique style that stands out from the rest of us. Her designs are kind of whimsical, but she definitely has an artist's eye.

This morning, I'm on my second breakfast cookie when Mom puts the lid back on the box and slides it off the counter away from me.

"Have a proper breakfast. I made eggs, bacon and toast. There's also a hash brown casserole warming in the oven."

I lean over and kiss her cheek. "Thanks, Mom."

I've finished breakfast by the time Elise and Luc make it to the kitchen. I glance up the stairs for Piper.

Luc puts some scrambled eggs and toast on a plate and sits down next to me.

"Where's your girl?"

He nods toward the stairs. "Still getting ready. You think you can keep up today?"

I scoff. "Are you really going to leave your girlfriend behind? Or is she as good as you?"

"No one in this house is as good as me."

Elise sits down next to me. "Which run are we taking first, Luc? Storm Peak? Three O'Clock? Or do you need to test your legs on something easier?"

"I don't need to warm up. How about Valley View to Lower Valley for a nice long run?"

She grins. "Sounds good to me. Mac, you in?"

It's been a few years since I've skied, but we grew up on these mountains, so I'm not worried. I could do most of the trails in the dark. However, the path Luc laid out isn't for beginners. I hope Piper has some experience with black diamonds.

Why am I even worried about her? She's not my girlfriend. It's Luc's job to make sure she can handle everything. I'm here to reconnect with my family and have some fun. Maybe spending time on the mountain and in town will help me feel good about coming back here to work. It's not the same as flying F-16s, but my adrenaline pumps pretty hard when I'm zipping down the side of a mountain. Not that I'll be doing that regularly in the role I'll be taking, but I don't really want to think about that right now, so I push the thought away and give my sister a nod. "Let's do it."

A stair creaks, and all three of us look over. Piper stops at the bottom of the staircase dressed in black leggings, a chunky gray sweater, and wool socks nearly up to her knees. Her long dark hair has been pulled back into French braids, and there's a small white smudge under one eye. She smiles at our table.

"Something sure smells good. What are we having?"

"Breakfast," Luc says, taking a bite of toast.

I tear my eyes away from Piper to glare at Luc. "She's your guest," I whisper, "why don't you fix her something?"

"Oh, yeah, sure." He quickly stands up. "Piper, can I make you a plate?"

She walks over to the kitchen island and surveys the contents. "I've got it, but thanks."

While she's getting her food, I clear my dishes, passing behind her and noticing she smells sweet, kind of like fresh-baked cookies. She turns to grab a mug from next to the coffeemaker, and I see the smudge on her face is sunscreen. Instinctively, I reach my hand up and rub it in. She freezes under my touch, her eyes widening. Realizing what I'm doing, I pull my hand away and take a big step back, hitting something. There's a crash behind me. I wince, turning to see I've made Elise drop her plate, which is now shattered on the floor.

"Sorry," I say, looking between Elise and Piper.

I grab the broom and dustpan from the mudroom and quickly sweep up the mess. When I'm finished, I head upstairs to get dressed for the slopes, trying to figure out what's gotten into me. I'm normally very aware of my surroundings. Something's got me a little off-kilter.

When I get back downstairs, everyone is standing by the back door, coats in hand. I grab mine, and we pick up our ski gear on our way out to the shuttle stop. We load ourselves and our gear onto the bus. Elise and I sit next to each other. Piper and Lucas are in the seats across the aisle.

"Guess you're my ski buddy today," Elise says to me, nodding over at the couple.

"Lucky me," I say.

She chuckles and knocks my shoulder with hers, then leans in to whisper. "Piper rented gear. Think she'll be able to keep up?"

I shrug. "Luc didn't seem concerned, and he should know."

"I should know what?" Luc says, meeting my gaze.

"Whether Piper can hang with us," Elise says.

"She's fine. Aren't you, Pipes?" he says, not breaking eye contact with me.

"Um, sure." She doesn't sound certain, so I end the staring contest, my gaze pinging over to Piper. She looks a little paler than usual. Or maybe I'm just imagining things.

When we're unloaded, we grab our skis and trek over to the Wild Blue Gondola for a breathtaking fifteen-minute ride up the slopes. The four of us get a car to ourselves. I'm seated across from Piper, who is staring open-mouthed at the snow and trees all around us.

"Have you been here before, Piper?" The opportunity to say her name gives me a small spark of pleasure.

She shakes her head without looking at me. I feel oddly disappointed.

"Where's the last place you skied?" Elise says.

"Um...I'm not sure."

Elise's forehead creases. "We can start on the blues if you'd prefer. We've got all day to get to the blacks."

I notice Luc stiffen next to Piper, but then he smiles, his body relaxing. He puts an arm casually behind Piper. "What do you think?"

She looks up at him and gives him a sweet smile. "I'll do what everyone else wants to do. Maybe you can go first and show me how it's done."

That makes Luc grin wider, his chest puffing out a bit. I guess Piper figured out that stroking his ego is the way to his heart. "Sure thing. Follow my lead, and you'll be fine."

I turn my head to hide my annoyance. I'm glad I'm not around my brother and his big head very often. His cockiness is bothering me more than usual this morning, but I can't put my finger on why.

We put our skis on at the top of the mountain and make sure helmets, goggles, gloves, and balaclavas cover all of our skin. Excitement zips through me in anticipation of flying down the mountain. Much as I may protest, I really do like spending time with my siblings. I love that we have skiing in common. Though it's pretty much impossible not to when you're part of our family.

"Should we go first?" Elise asks me.

I shake my head, the protector in me wanting to see how everyone fares on the first run and being ready to help as needed. A small part of me also doesn't want to be out front where people can watch me wobble as I get my snow legs under me.

Luc checks over Piper's equipment before giving her a thumbs up, which she returns. I'm glad he's finally looking after her. Probably reminds him of our ski instructor days. All three of us kids spent at least one season teaching newbies the ropes. Luc turns his skis and starts down the mountain, making wide turns that become narrower as his muscle memory returns.

Piper's mumbling something as she uses her poles to tip over the edge. She picks up speed quickly as she zips straight down the hill. She lets out a sharp yelp, her skis wobbling, before she wipes out.

I'm skidding to a stop just above her before I even realize I've moved. I unclip my skis and am on my knees on the snow next to the motionless woman.

"Piper. Are you hurt? Can you tell me what happened?"

"Too many French fries and not enough pizza."

Did she hit her head? The helmet is supposed to protect her, but that fall looked rough. Plus, she's not making any sense. "Do you need a snack?"

Her laugh is strangled, like she's lost her breath.

Elise stops next to me. "Everything okay?"

"I'm not sure."

Piper waves a hand at Elise. "I'll be fine. Nothing's hurt but my pride."

"Can you stand up?"

I take her gloved hand with mine and lever her up. I can't even see her eyes through her goggles, and everything else is covered, so there's no way to assess injuries.

"Really, guys," Piper says, "I'm good. Go on without me. I'll catch up. Eventually."

There's no way I'm leaving a possibly concussed woman alone at the top of the mountain. Especially since Lucas is nowhere to be seen. He's probably near Four Points Lodge by now. I turn to Elise.

"Can you go down and find Luc? Tell him we're coming, but it may be a while."

"I can stay and help," she says.

"No, no," Piper says. "I don't want to ruin everyone's day because I'm a little clumsy. I can get down on my own."

I shake my head. "Not gonna happen. Elise, go." The authority in my voice leaves no room for further debate.

She heads off without another word, leaving the two of us.

"Let me help you to your feet," I say, reaching for her hands again. She takes them and tries to get up before her skis are turned perpendicular to the fall line, causing her to slide further downhill and right into my torso.

This sets off another warning bell in my brain. "How long has it been since you skied?"

She coughs. "Uh, thirty years or so."

"You're thirty," I deadpan.

"Yep," she squeaks.

"You've never skied before?"

"You got me."

I grab her shoulders and pull her away, then silently curse the reflective lenses of her goggles covering her eyes. "Why on earth would you agree to go down black diamonds when you don't know how to ski?"

"It's just snow, right? It can't hurt that much. Besides, I've done other winter sports. I thought some skills might transfer over."

Her argument almost sounds reasonable, but I can't think of anything other than water skiing that might be useful, and that's definitely not a winter sport. That Luc obviously had no knowledge of Piper's skill level makes me irrationally angry with him. She could have seriously injured herself, and all because she's apparently trying to impress my dumb brother, who disappeared down the hill without a backward glance.

"What sports?"

"Sledding, obviously."

I shake my head. "Not a sport."

"And ice skating." She raises her chin in a way that makes me think she's glaring at me. "And before you say that's not a sport, you have to skate to play hockey."

"Still not sure how that would help with skiing."

She sighs. "Okay, maybe not perfect logic, but I did at least Google ski basics. I just didn't realize my brain would freeze up when I saw the size of the mountain."

It sounds like I'm going to be giving a private lesson as we work our way down. Let's see what I'm working with. "What did you learn from the internet?"

"To go downhill, pretend like your skis are two French fries. If you want to stop, put them together like a wedge of pizza. I definitely got the fries down, but trying the pizza made me nervous about crossing skis, and I've read that's how you tear your ACL or break a leg."

I silently curse Luc for this terrible oversight on his part. How has the conversation of skiing experience not come up once in their dating relationship? It better not be because he's spent the whole time basking in Piper's adoration of him and not bothering to learn much about her in return. My teeth clench, and I have to force my jaw to relax so I can respond. "You're right. You don't want to cross your ski tips, but the trick with pizza is pushing your heels out. That's what slows you down. As does making wide turns in the snow. I know it can be a little intimidating, but it's easier on your legs. If you try to plow all the way down to the bottom, your quads will be shot before you even reach the first lodge."

"So what do I do?"

"I'm going to give you a lesson. Thankfully, we're still on Traverse which has flattened out." For now.

She swallows thickly. "This isn't steep?"

"It's no bunny trail like you ought to be on, but it's wide enough that you can make slow turns."

I spend the next few minutes talking her through what we need to do. I wish I had my guide rope so I could strap her to me, but I'll just have to hope she's a fast learner. When the only thing left to do is go through the motions, I put on my skis and instruct her to follow me. I ski nearly perpendicular to the mountain before making a wide arc and stopping facing the other way. She pushes off from the other side and glides slowly toward me. I try to mind-meld with her to turn her left ski in and around to face the other way. She starts off well, but I see the moment she freaks out about facing downhill again. Before I can react, she slams into me, and we both go down.

Chapter Nine

Piper

My life flashes before my eyes at the moment of impact. My body hits what feels like a concrete wall, and I'm shocked when it topples over, me falling with it. The breath goes out of Mac as he hits the snow, and I land on top of his very firm torso. Even through both of our coats, I can feel the firmness of his stomach muscles.

I scramble off of him as quickly as possible, which is very challenging with two skis strapped to my feet.

"Did I hurt you?"

"I'm good," he croaks out.

The only thing not covered is his lips, and I can't help staring at them. They're different from Lucas's. Lucas has a very pronounced cupid's bow, while Mac's lips are soft and plump, like new pillows. I blink to derail this train of thought. I definitely shouldn't be thinking about my boyfriend's brother's lips. Okay, so he's my *fake* boyfriend, but if I'm successful with my plan, we'll be dating for real by the new year.

My idea of dazzling Lucas with my ski skills is obviously a flop. It seems delusional now to think I could simply figure it out on the fly. In my defense, it looked pretty easy on the videos I watched. I expected Mac to yell at me, or at least laugh at my stupidity, when I told him I'd never skied before. I hoped that making it a joke might diffuse some tension, but he was very calm and matter-of-fact in his responses. I suppose being an Air Force pilot requires keeping a tight hold on your emotions and reactions.

Instead of receiving a dressing down I totally deserve, he's actually trying to teach me the skills I need to make it safely down the mountain. Though if I keep up my current progress, it'll be Mac with most of the injuries.

I was feeling a little confident sliding along the side of the mountain, but as soon as I turned downhill, I flashed back to my earlier out-of-control careening and panicked. Right into Mac. I feel terrible about everything. I'm ruining his family ski day. If we ever make it down the mountain, I'll spend the rest of the day in the lodge by a fire while the siblings enjoy the snow. Because this will be my first and last time skiing. It's more terrifying than I imagined.

After Mac regains his breath, he helps me back up to a standing position.

"That wasn't too bad. You almost made a complete turn. Let's go slow back across and try it again."

I let out a disbelieving scoff. "You really think we should keep going? I could kill you."

"There's only one way down the mountain. Well, two. Ski patrol could come get you in their sled, but that's mostly for people who can't get down themselves."

Understanding makes me shiver with trepidation. What have I gotten myself into? "You mean people with broken bones."

"Among other things. Look, you seem athletic. Let's get your turns down and I'll navigate you down the mountain. Eventually, we'll be able to take blues and greens down to the square."

Part of me feels like I should be insulted he wants to take me the easier route, even though it's the most logical solution. The other part is grateful we can avoid the hardest trails. If I'm on a medium one now, I can't imagine what hard looks like. Regardless, it sounds like I'd better figure out this turning thing because I'm going to be doing it a lot.

"Okay. For what it's worth, I'm sorry I've ruined family ski day. When we get to the bottom, I'll find somewhere to hang out, and the rest of you can ski together."

He's quiet for a moment. "Let's get to the bottom first. Think you can follow me again?"

"Yes, but I can't guarantee I won't knock you over."

"I'll brace myself this time."

His lips tip up slightly, letting me know he's teasing. I smile, even though my mouth is covered by cloth. With as serious as Mac has been, I expected him to be all business. This gentle ribbing is a pleasant surprise.

This time skiing across Storm Peak, I give myself a pep talk that I won't freak and will see my turn through. Amazingly, it works. My arc is wider than Mac's, and I end up a few yards down the mountain from him. He gives me a thumbs up, which I mirror back in case he's making sure I'm okay. I watch him cut a lazy path across the slope and make another graceful turn. I turn my skis enough to start sliding and play out my future turn in my head. It goes a little better than the previous one, and I'm only a few feet past Mac this time. We continue to play follow the leader until we come to a wooden lodge with "Four Points" on the side in large white letters.

Mac pulls his mask down under his chin and sets his goggles on top of his head so I can see his entire face. I do the same, breathing steadily from our exertion. My leg muscles are a little sore, but not completely used up yet.

"Congratulations. You've made it a third of the way down the mountain."

"*What*?!" I yelp. "I feel like we've been up here forever."

He slides his phone out of his coat pocket. "It's been about an hour and a half."

My mouth drops open. "That's all? At this rate, it's going to take us all day to get to the bottom."

"Isn't that the point?"

"I suppose, but I don't think my legs are going to last me another three hours. This is hard work."

"If you'd prefer, I can get you over to Thunderhead Lodge in an hour or so, and then we can take a gondola back to the square."

My pride wants me to tough it out and ski all the way down, but I don't think my body will hold up as long as I'd need it to. Still, I don't want to give up just yet. I feel quite accomplished having made it this far, seeing as it's my first time skiing.

"Let's play it by ear."

He nods. "Do you need the bathroom or food?"

I'd like nothing more than to sit down and drink some cocoa, but I know if I take all of this gear off, it's going to be very hard to convince myself to put it back on. I shake my head. "Let's keep going."

He stares at me for a few beats, as if he's assessing whether to press the issue. "Alright. We have a choice to make. We can either take another blue trail or a longer green one that's a more gradual descent."

Hmm, do I want an easier trail or a shorter trail? My legs beg for easy. "Let's do the green one."

We navigate around some people to the back side of the building and start down a trail called Chisolm, which is bordered by trees. The branches, heavy with snow, make me feel like I'm in a veritable wonderland. Mac was right. This slope is much less scary than what we were doing. It allows me to take in the scenery more fully instead of having to stay solely focused on my skis and the few feet of snow in front of me. I feel somewhat graceful making my turns and gliding across the snow. I can almost see why people enjoy this sport.

Mac stops at a sharp bend in the path and waits for me. I manage to stop before I run into him again.

"How are we doing?"

I'm humored at his use of "we" like we're a team. "*I'm* doing pretty well, but I bet this is boring for you."

He shakes his head. "It's been a long time since I was on this trail. I'm enjoying being able to take in the views rather than look out for people below while racing my siblings to the bottom. It's an adrenaline rush for sure, but you miss how beautiful everything is."

I don't think his words are for my sake. They sound genuine. It's nice that he appreciates how incredible our surroundings are. "Yeah, it is pretty amazing up here. The crisp, clean air with a hint of pine trees. It smells like Christmas."

That elicits a small smile from him. "Are you a big fan of Christmas?"

I purse my lips, my mood sinking. "I used to be. Not so much recently."

I brace myself for awkward follow-up questions that don't come.

"I haven't really done much celebrating lately either. It's a bit of a holiday overload coming back here."

Relieved I don't have to explain myself, I nod, understanding what he means. The house is decorated to the nines with garland, lights, and Christmas kitsch. I think there's a tree in every room. Our bedroom has a tiny plastic tree sitting on the dresser with pint-sized ornaments to match. While inviting, it also overwhelms the senses a bit.

"Are the houses up here decorated for Christmas year-round?"

A laugh rumbles in his chest. "Surprisingly, no. Mom does everything in early November. A few years ago she took pictures and gave each room its own box to make things easier for her."

The family must rent the same house every year if she's set up a storage system. Or maybe they own it. If you have enough money, I suppose you can afford to have a separate vacation home. I want to ask Mac about it but keep my mouth shut because this sounds like something Lucas's girlfriend would already know.

I take a deep breath, closing my eyes and enjoying just being outside in all this beauty. I hear a whoosh and open my eyes as a family zooms past us in the snow.

"I guess we should continue on," I say, reluctant to leave this winter paradise.

"We're skiing over to Burgess Creek Lift, which will take us to Thunderhead Lodge, where we'll take a break and get something to drink. How does that sound?"

"Pretty good except for one thing."

"What's that?"

"I've never been on a ski lift before."

He smiles in a way I think is meant to reassure me. Instead, my stomach flops nervously.

"It's pretty easy. Just ski up to the line when it's our turn and sit down for a nice break. You're not afraid of heights, are you?"

I give him a wry smile. "Today would cure me of my fear if I were. We weren't exactly skimming the ground in the gondola."

He nods, then turns and starts slowly down the hill. Mac has the patience of a saint. I bet he's secretly champing at the bit to go flying and leave me in the dust, but he's hiding it well. When we reach the lift, we're able to ski right on. Mac motions taking the pole straps off my wrists and clasping them together in one hand. When we're comfortably seated on the lift, he pulls down the safety bar and we zip up the mountain, legs dangling. I'm initially worried my skis will fall off, but they stay secured to my boots the whole trip. When we get close to the end of the lift, Mac pushes the bar back up and leans toward me.

"At the top, lean forward and kind of crouch off the lift, letting yourself glide on the skis."

I do what he says and manage not to fall. I almost feel like a real skier. After re-looping my poles to my wrists, I follow Mac down a short path to a gigantic lodge. He suggests we take a break and get some water. It's obvious the rest is for my benefit, and my leg muscles scream at me to accept the offer.

Mac helps me out of my skis, stacking them together and sticking them in a storage slot along with his skis and our poles. We walk inside, taking off our helmets and gloves and lowering our masks as we go. He leads me over to a bar with an enormous wall of windows showing the snowy mountainside.

"We started all the way up there," he says, pointing.

I almost can't believe my eyes. "No way."

"You did amazingly well for your first time."

I grimace. "Again, I'm sorry. I didn't realize just how challenging it would be. I pictured something like that last trail in my head. Long, but not too steep. That was actually pretty enjoyable."

"Those trails are what you're *supposed* to start on. They're confidence builders that help you solidify your skills for the steeper terrain."

"That makes sense. Hey, if you want to catch up with Lucas and Elise, I can probably get myself the rest of the way down."

He shakes his head. "I texted them when we were at Four Points and told them to go on together. We'll all ski together another day."

I hate that my stupidity has thwarted Mac's plans for the day. He shouldn't be babysitting me. If anyone should be here, it should be Lucas. I grab my phone but have no texts or missed calls. I know we're not really dating, but I'd think he'd at least check in to see how I'm doing. His inaction annoys me a little, but I stuff it down. It's not his fault I can't ski. I should have just been honest from the beginning, even if it meant sitting at home with his parents all day. At least I would be less sore and in no position to physically harm another person. I'm definitely a danger on the slopes—to myself and others. Especially Mac. "Are you sure? I feel bad ruining your family fun."

"It's fine."

He doesn't seem annoyed, but he probably just hides it well.

"I'm really sorry about body slamming you earlier. I hope you don't have any bruises."

"Stop apologizing. We're good. I'm glad you're a fast learner."

"Only because you're a very good on-the-fly instructor."

He huffs out a breath. "I should be. I gave lessons for several years in high school."

"Really? Where?"

He looks at me strangely. "Here."

That's right. His family has money. Of course, they'd have spent a lot of time here since Lucas was a Junior Olympic skier. I just assumed his family was from Denver since that's where Lucas lives, but the house feels very lived in. And Mac said something about moving back here at dinner last night. Am I staying in the family home? Mrs. Cahill's storage boxes make a lot more sense if that's the case.

"Did you grow up here?"

"Yeeessss. Just like Luc." He gives me a questioning look.

The way he drew out his affirmation makes me feel like I should know this. I guess it is kind of weird I don't know this about Lucas. I shake my head. I need to be more careful with my questions. Too many, and it'll be very clear Lucas and I are practically strangers. Time to play dumb.

"Oh, duh. I forgot for a second you're Lucas's brother. You two look nothing alike."

He nods. "We get that a lot. Luc looks like Dad, and I take after Mom. People used to ask if one of us was adopted."

I frown. "Well, that's mean."

He shrugs. "I'm hungry. You?"

My stomach growls in response, and I pat it. "There's your answer."

We grab slices of pizza and sodas. Mac chats with the people behind the counter and high-fives the guy working the register. "Todd, great to see you. How's the season going?"

"Better than last year, Mr. Cahill."

Mac shakes his head. "Just Mac. Keep up the great work."

We find seats and devour our food.

"I'm still hungry. You want another slice?" Mac asks, eyeing my empty plate.

"Sure, but I'll get it. You paid for the last ones."

He gives me a weird look. "Actually, I didn't. You want another pepperoni?" I nod. "Be right back."

While he's gone, I mentally replay Mac's interaction with the guy at checkout. He knew his name and was called Mr. Cahill. And now that I think about it, he definitely didn't pull out a wallet. Goosebumps rise on my arms as I realize something's off. Pulling out my phone, I type in "Cahill family Steamboat Springs" and click on the first link. The page informs me that the Cahill family has run the mountain resort for over sixty years. The Cahill name even goes back to the founding of the town in 1900. Oh. No wonder they're all skiing pros. How did this info not get into

Lucas's emails? We're going to have a little chat when I see him next.

I pocket my phone just as Mac returns.

"Thanks," I say, taking the slice. Part of me wants to ask about his role in the family business, but it's probably something I should talk to Lucas about. Just to avoid any potential landmines. Who knows if there's any family drama.

After we eat, Mac leads me out onto a deck with a metal sculpture shaped like a picture frame for a photo. It's super touristy, but I'm obviously a tourist. He snaps a picture of me with his phone.

"Let's take one together."

He frowns. "Why?"

"So I can show all my friends the man who kept me from killing myself today."

Another guest offers to take it, so we stand next to each other. I smile, hoping Mac is doing the same. When she extends the phone to Mac, I grab it and text the photos to myself, then hand it over. I pull my phone out to make sure the text came through. I laugh when I see Mac isn't smiling in the second photo. Perfect. I text it to Christy.

After heading back outside to grab our gear, we load up in the gondola for the ride back to the base of the mountain. My phone vibrates, and I pull it out.

Christy: Who's that scowling man?

Piper: Lucas's brother, Mac. He helped me survive my first time skiing.

Christy: Is this the same brother you flirted with?

Piper: Yes. *cringe face emoji*

Christy: I don't blame you. That man is hot. *hot face emoji* Did he have to give you mouth-to-mouth?

Piper: No. You can't drown in snow.

Christy: What a shame.

I try to hold in my laughter, but a snort escapes. Mac looks over at me, and I hit the lock button on my phone and stuff it into my pocket. It vibrates again, and I pull it out to see who it's from, worried it might be Christy with more inappropriate comments. Instead, it's a message from one of my weekend art students.

I've held free classes for high school students on Saturday mornings for several years. It's a great outlet for them and for me. Graphic design isn't as fulfilling as I'd hoped it'd be, so I've had to get creative. Teaching is not quite the same as being a full-time artist, but that dream disintegrated years ago.

I slide my phone back into my pocket, knowing it probably isn't urgent. Most messages are photos of projects they've finished.

I'll look at it later when I can properly study the image and give detailed feedback.

I feel eyes on me and look over just as Mac's head twists away to look out the window. Was Mac just staring at me? He's probably wondering how someone could be so brazen as to think they could conquer a mountain on the first try. Well, I won't make that mistake again.

I turn away and look out my side of the gondola, startled to see a statue of a clown sitting on an old chairlift. Is that Ronald McDonald? I blink to make sure my eyes aren't playing tricks on me, but it's still there. I peer over at Mac, ready to ask him about it, but his head is against his window and his eyes are closed. He probably has a headache from dealing with my shenanigans, so I leave him be. I should find a way to make it up to him for this morning. I'm sure he'd much rather have been anywhere else but inching down the snow with me.

Chapter Ten

Mac

It's obvious Piper won't be doing any more skiing today. Maybe never, depending on how traumatized she is by her first experience. I'm angry with Luc for putting her in that position and am doing my best not to take it out on the person sitting next to me. He should have known she was a novice and taken time to show her the basics, even if it meant having to wait to tackle his favorite runs. It's what you do when you're in a relationship. In the six months they've been together, I'd have thought he'd realized everything's not about him, but perhaps Piper defers to him and keeps her own desires to herself. The thought makes me even angrier. If Luc isn't going to be a good boyfriend, perhaps he shouldn't be in a relationship. I can't believe I might have to sit him down and remind him how women should be treated. Unfortunately, it's going to be awhile before I can do that because it sounds like he intends to stay on the slopes all day. Which may be for the best, because if I saw him right now, I'd probably throttle him.

Has Luc even checked in on Piper? He hasn't answered any of my calls or texts. At least Elise is in communication. She asked how Piper was doing, which I hope was because Luc asked, but I'm doubtful. Piper insisted I tell Elise they should enjoy themselves and not worry about her. Guess that leaves me to do the worrying.

I like what little I know about Piper. She's obviously a talented graphic designer if her cookies represent her artistic abilities. And she has grit, evidenced by her determination to learn enough skills to get down the mountain with her own strength. It isn't easy figuring things out on the side of a giant mountain. I really was worried we'd have to contact ski patrol, but she proved me wrong.

However, the fact that I don't know her means I could be casting her in some rosy glow she doesn't deserve. She was texting with someone who made her smile and laugh. Even though I wasn't trying to snoop, I saw a message from someone named Sam. There was a heart emoji after his name, which leaves some uneasy questions in my brain. Is she flirting with another man while dating my brother? Or worse? She doesn't seem like the type, or maybe I just hope she isn't. I won't jump to conclusions, mainly because it's not any of my business. Though if she does like someone else, it might explain why she doesn't seem very concerned about Luc's neglect. Maybe she's just stringing him along. For what purpose, I have no idea. This line of thinking is souring my mood even more than it already was. For all I know, Luc and Piper could be very happy together, and I'm just making up a bunch of nonsense.

Like I said, it's none of my business. I need to remember that.

What *is* my business is making sure Piper's alright and keeping her entertained until her boyfriend returns. Okay, no one has assigned this job to me, but making sure everyone is happy is kind of my thing. I've been doing it since I was little, and there's no reason to stop now.

The gondola stops at the base of the mountain, and we unload.

"Do you want to go back to the house?"

She fidgets with her fingers. "Yeah, probably. I'm definitely not going back up the mountain, but you should join your siblings. I can find my way back to the house."

I'm sure she's a capable person who could get there on her own just fine, but I'd have more peace of mind seeing her get there myself. Besides, I'm still so riled up about the day's events, my brother and I would be in a wrestling match on the side of the mountain the moment I saw him. The smart thing to do is to take more time to calm down.

"I'll go with you. I wouldn't mind getting warmed up again."

We pick up our skis and head over to the shuttle area. This time I notice how awkward she is walking in ski boots. No one looks cool in them, but she walks like a baby deer trying out its legs for the first time. It's actually kind of cute. I take her skis from her, wondering why I didn't offer earlier. I'm slipping. A sign I haven't spent much time in the company of a woman lately. Some of my co-workers are women, but they'd see it as condescending if I showed them preferential treatment.

After we remove our outer clothes and hang them up in the garage, we traipse through the mudroom to the kitchen. Mom already has snacks out on the kitchen counter. She stands up from her chair in the living room and comes over.

"You're back early." She looks past me into the mudroom. "Where are the others?"

"They're still on the mountain. We decided we'd had enough skiing for one day."

Piper raises her hand. "It's my fault, actually. Everyone else is way out of my league skill-wise. Mac was gracious enough to stay with me and make sure I didn't hurt myself or someone else. Though we weren't completely successful on that front."

She shoots me a playful smile, and I have to press my lips together to keep from grinning. I know she's thinking about when she slammed into me, because that memory is seared into my brain. Who knew such a small person could pack a huge wallop? Ending up on my back was a big surprise, though it's hard to really get hurt in powder two feet deep while dressed like the Stay Puft Marshmallow Man.

"Oh no, what happened?"

"Nothing. Everyone's fine." I nod toward the stove. "Is that your famous hot cocoa?"

Mom smiles. "You know it. Grab a mug, and I'll get out the marshmallows and whipped cream."

Piper catches my eye and raises an eyebrow. "Marshmallows?"

I shrug. "Just because we're adults doesn't mean we can't indulge in some childhood joy."

She considers that and then nods. "In that case, do you have any powdered cinnamon, Mrs. Cahill?"

"It's Susie, hon. And of course. How else are we supposed to make fresh gingerbread for our house competition?"

Piper's eyes sparkle with excitement. "Ooh, when are we doing that?"

"Since you won last night's competition, you get to choose whether we build snowmen or make gingerbread houses tonight."

She rubs her hands together, looking pleased. "Those both sound like fun, but why not make today all about snow with skiing and snowmen?"

"Then that's what we'll do."

While the women are chatting, I fill two mugs with cocoa, leaving room for marshmallows. I hand the steaming mug with Santa's face to Piper, then set my reindeer mug on the counter and peruse the options. Mini marshmallows, regular marshmallows, chocolate shavings, mini candy canes, caramel sauce, whipped cream in a can, sprinkles, and a shaker of cinnamon.

"Ladies first," I say, curious to see what Piper does.

She grins, then puts in five mini marshmallows, fills the mug with whipped cream until she's made a small mountain, and then shakes cinnamon over the cream.

"Why cinnamon?"

"Try it and find out."

I top my cocoa just like hers, except I add a few chocolate shavings to the whipped cream at the end. When I pick up my cup, Piper clinks hers to mine.

"Cheers."

She drags her tongue through the whipped cream and cinnamon. I chuckle at the small dot of cream on her nose.

"You missed a little," I say, rubbing the end of my nose.

She sticks out her tongue and tries to reach her nose unsuccessfully. She looks at me and laughs at whatever expression is on my face.

"I keep hoping that one day I'll be able to touch my nose with my tongue. Today is obviously not that day."

She wipes the cream off with her finger and sticks it in her mouth. I shake my head, amused by her antics. She seems much too silly for Luc. He doesn't like looking foolish in anything. But maybe that's what he likes about her. I could probably use someone in my life who encourages me to have more fun. Why not have a little fun right now?

I stick out my tongue and run it through my whipped cream like Piper. The cinnamon, whipped cream, and chocolate combination is delicious and tastes like Christmas.

"You're right. That's good."

"Thank you. So what should we do now?"

"You can work on the puzzle," Mom says, nodding toward the sitting room where a card table is set up.

I grab two sugar cookies out of the container and give one to Piper when we reach the table. Part of the border has been constructed, but that's it. It's nothing but candy canes. I groan. This is going to be tough. At least a few candy canes have a green stripe, so those should be easier to find.

By the time Luc and Elise return to the house, we've finished the border and assembled a few complete candy canes. Truth be told, Piper's the one who put together the inner candy canes. She's much better at this than I am. I've resorted to looking for odd-shaped pieces I can fill in because the colors of the pieces all look the same to me. Meanwhile, she snaps pieces into place with ease.

"How in the world are you doing that? Are you some sort of puzzle savant?"

She smiles. "No. Look. This one has more purple tones in the shadows, while that one is more green."

I blink at her, seeing no difference. "Are you just making that up?"

She laughs. "Must be my art-trained eyes."

Luc walks over. "The powder today was sick! We must have hit twenty runs."

Aaaand my anger is back. I grit my teeth to tamp it down. "Yes, Piper is okay. Thanks for checking on her."

His smile drops, and he looks over at Piper. "I'm so glad. I didn't realize you weren't ready for blacks."

She places a hand on his shoulder. "No, it's my fault. I should have been honest about my experience. I'm glad you had a good time. I've enjoyed myself as well."

How in the world can she say that when she spent half of it tensely traversing a mountain? Especially when she could have been seriously injured. Still, it's not my place to interfere in someone else's relationship. I just need to keep my mouth shut. I get up from the table, grab our empty mugs, and stick them in the dishwasher. Mom is prepping dinner, so I ask her what I can do and get lost in the work. After dinner is over and cleaned up, we gather in the living room to prepare for the evening's activity.

"Piper has chosen the snowman competition for tonight," Mom says. "Nana and I will be the judges this evening. Luc and Piper, you two pair up. The rest of you will get your partners from the hat."

She pulls a Santa hat from behind her back and holds it out to Nana. She draws out two names.

"John and Mac."

"Which means Elise is with me," Dad says.

Uncle John smacks me on the shoulder. "Think we've got a chance, kid?"

I nod, already brainstorming what we should do.

"You will have one hour," Mom says. "Scarves, gloves, and such are in the green bin in the garage. You can use whatever else you find. Everyone gear up and head out to the backyard."

The floodlights are on out back, illuminating the pristine snow. I pause to appreciate it, knowing the backyard is about to get very messy. Mom and Nana stand on the second-floor balcony. Our three teams are standing in evenly spaced rows. Elise and Dad are in between my team and Luc's. It's probably for the best as last time we held this competition, Luc tried to sabotage my team by stealing the sticks we collected for arms.

"Ready...go!"

Uncle John and I roll snowballs for the body. We'll gather decorations once we have a strong snowball canvas to work with. After half an hour, we have all three pieces securely attached to one another. Our snowman looks like it's leaning a little, but we'll use that as part of our design. I can already see an older man with a cane, his other hand holding his aching back. I whisper my idea to Uncle John, who nods in agreement. I go inside to see if there's a suitable hat in the bin while Uncle John heads to the woods behind the house for sticks. On my way back to our snowman, I pass the others. Whatever Luc and Piper are making, it's not a traditional snowman. It's a squat, squarish design. I guess we'll see what the judges think. Elise and Dad's snowman looks unbalanced with the largest snowball on top. I have no idea what their strategy is.

Uncle John has planted a thick stick with a hook on the end in the snow for our snowman's cane and is working on locking it into place with the snowman's stick arm. I set the cap I found on the guy's head, wrap the plaid vest around the torso, then pull out a carrot and pipe from my jacket pocket. I carve out a hole for the carrot and draw a straight line for a mouth. We need eyes, so I search the woods until I find two little pine cones. Uncle John has the other arm in, and the old man looks almost exactly how I pictured him in my head.

"Five minutes," Mom calls from the balcony.

We use the time to define the man's features a little more. When Mom and Nana appear in the yard and call time, we all step away from our designs. I glance over and huff out a laugh when I see Dad and Elise's upside-down snowman. It's doing a headstand, its booted legs splayed in the air. Very creative. I peer past them, but can't tell what Luc and Piper made. From this angle, it looks sort of like a house with a weird-looking chimney. No hat, scarf, or stick hands to be seen. When Nana sees their design and chuckles, I'm very tempted to march over and see what it is, but tradition keeps me rooted next to my snowman until the winner is announced.

When the judges reach us at the end of the line, Nana raises her hand to her mouth, her face crumpling a little. "It looks just like Harry," she says. "That's his hat, you know."

I didn't know, but now I feel guilty for making Nana sad. Uncle John reaches out and hugs his mother. She gives him a squeeze and then pats his back until he lets her go.

Mom and Nana move away to confer with one another. After a few minutes, they turn and face the anxious crowd. Or maybe it's just me who's anxious. Though I notice Luc fidgeting down at the end of the row.

"This was tough," Nana says. "All the designs were great. Second place goes to John and Mac for their Grandpa design. Very spot on, you two. Our winners for tonight are...Luc and Piper!"

Luc picks Piper up in a hug and spins her around. I walk over to get a good look at what beat out our snowman. As I get closer, the design becomes clear. It's Snoopy the dog lying on top of his doghouse. His nose is a pinecone, and his ears are leaves. There are tiny sticks for his closed eyes. Beside the house is his water bowl with a little Woodstock skating on the frozen water. How in the world did they make that? The answer is obvious. Piper. At this rate, she's guaranteed to win the gingerbread house competition. Which means Luc will win again because he'll obviously be her partner. It's almost like cheating, except I can't be mad about her artistic talent. It's not her I'm mad at, anyway.

"That's amazing," I say.

"Thanks," Luc says, setting Piper down. "My girlfriend and I make an amazing team."

I close my eyes to keep from rolling them. "But it's not a snowman." I turn to Nana. "I thought this was a *snowman*-building competition?"

She just shrugs and pats my arm. "Sometimes we need a little change. We can either fight it or enjoy it."

I harrumph, even though the only reason I care about who won is because I hate hearing Luc gloat.

"Great job, everyone," Mom says. "Now come inside and warm up."

"I have a better idea," Luc says. "Let's get in the hot tub."

The idea of sharing a hot tub with my brother and his girlfriend is not very appealing.

Luc gives Piper his most charming smile. "What do you think?"

She smiles up at him, making my stomach twist. "Sounds perfect."

"I'll pass," I say, "but you two have fun."

"Oh, we will," Luc says, grinning at Piper. "Don't you worry."

Chapter Eleven

Piper

The thought of spending some time alone with Lucas is both exciting and a little nerve-racking. I mean, it's the first time we've really been alone this trip, and I'm going to be doing it in my swimsuit. Christy talked me into going for the wow factor over comfort. Now that I'm here where it's nearing zero degrees outside, I'm rethinking the plan to show so much skin. I rustle in my bag for a pair of thick wool socks to warm up my numb toes on the cold wood floor. I didn't think to bring a cover-up, but I spy a plaid robe in the closet and snuggle into it. It's flannel and looks like it's been around for a while, but it does the trick, falling almost to my ankles. I cinch the belt around my waist and use the mirror to put my hair up into a messy topknot. Wet hair out in the cold is not my idea of a good time.

When I pass through the living room, I feel eyes on me, but I keep going, knowing I probably look ridiculous in the too-big robe and socks. When I get out to the deck, Lucas is already in the tub, his back to me. There are two towels on a nearby chair. The sound of the sliding door closing must alert him to my presence because he turns. His lips press together while he gives me a once-over in my getup.

I take off my socks and stuff them in the pockets of the robe, then uncinch the belt and slide it off my shoulders. The smirk on Lucas's face changes. He does another slow perusal of my body as I hang the robe over the back of the chair and slide into the tub across from him.

"Whoa, Piper. I didn't realize you were so hot. Your office sweaters really don't do you justice."

My cheeks warm at his appreciative gaze. He motions for me to come closer to him. I slide around the side of the tub. He continues waving his hand until I'm seated right next to him and he puts an arm around my shoulder.

"I thought you didn't want to do a lot of PDA," I say softly, even though I'm pretty sure we're alone.

"What kind of guy would I be if I didn't warm up my girlfriend? Especially after she helped us win the snowman competition? Besides," he says, lowering his voice, "I'm pretty sure we're being watched through the glass doors behind us."

I stiffen, not having considered that. Is his family looking at us? I want to turn my head to check, but I shouldn't be worried about them. My focus should be on taking advantage of the situation. I relax my body and snuggle into Lucas, letting my head drop onto his shoulder.

"I *am* pretty cold. Your hot tub idea is perfect."

"I agree."

His arm slides down my back to rest on my hip. I have to force my body not to tense up. You'd think I'd be melting into him, having imagined scenarios like this for the past three years, but now that it's happening, it doesn't quite feel right. Maybe it's the thought of being observed. Mentally, I try to shake my discomfort.

"I'm sorry about today. I know I should have told you I didn't know how to ski, but I didn't want to let you down. I don't remember you mentioning in our emails that your family owns the resort."

"No, I'm sorry. I shouldn't have assumed anything. I also should have been more forthcoming about my family."

"Are you going to work here someday?"

I feel his neck move against my temple as he shakes his head. "No. My family hoped all of us kids would join the resort in some capacity. It's why I went to business school, but I really want to do my own thing. Stand on my own feet, you know?"

I can see how someone like Lucas wouldn't want to disappear into someone else's dream. He likes to stand out, be the top dog. And he has the talent to back it up. I can't really fault him. "What about your siblings?"

"Mac's stint in the Air Force is about finished, and then Dad expects him to take over. Elise is currently working in hospitality at the resort, but I'm pretty sure her eye is on management."

"Well, at least you have a family who supports you and loves you no matter what."

"They don't seem to understand my drive and work ethic, though. Mom thinks I work too much, but I love what I do. Closing a huge deal gives me such a high that all the hard work and extra hours are more than worth it. Yes, sometimes that means working over holidays, but it doesn't bother me, and it's my life. Shouldn't they just be happy that I'm happy?"

I'm surprised Lucas is opening up to me like this. I knew he was a hard worker, but I didn't realize he got so much flak from his family about it. He just needs someone who understands him and will support him. Someone who won't try to clip his wings. I can show him I'd be a great addition to his life by offering my unwavering support for his career.

I lift my head from his shoulder and meet his gaze. "It's your life, Lucas. I'm impressed with your ambition and strong work ethic. You should surround yourself with people who lift you up rather than try to tie you down and fit you into their mold."

He gives me an appreciative smile that makes my heart skip a beat. His eyes roam my face like he's really taking me in. They pause briefly on my lips, and my breath catches. "You're right. I need someone who really understands me. Who sees me and accepts me as I am. Thanks, Piper."

"You're welcome." My words come out a little shaky. I hope he doesn't notice.

"So listen…" He pauses.

There are so many things that could finish that sentence. Is Lucas gearing up to say he thinks we should make this fake thing real? I wouldn't be opposed to that. It'd give me a chance to see if his kisses are just as devastating as his smiles.

"There's a chance I may have to go back to Denver the day after tomorrow. I'm so close to landing this deal I've been working on. The client has a few follow-up questions, and I'd like to reassure them in person. Would you be all right staying here with my family by yourself? I'd probably be back by dinner."

The hope in my chest plummets to my feet. That wasn't what I was expecting, but it's an opportunity to show my support for his career. It feels like a test. One I can pass, even if it may be a little awkward being alone with a bunch of strangers. Though his family has been so warm and inviting to me, I doubt it'll be much of a hardship. I'll work on the puzzle, read a book, or take a walk.

"Sure, no problem. Do what you've got to do."

He grins, then leans in and presses a kiss to my forehead. "Thanks. You're the best fake girlfriend I've ever had."

His words knot my stomach. I'm going to have to work harder to rid him of the notion that this should only be a temporary arrangement. Unfortunately, I don't have a lot of ideas at the moment.

Lucas releases his hold on my waist and stands up. "I'm pruning, so it's time to get out."

I guess our moment's over. Lucas steps out of the hot tub and grabs a towel. I watch him dry off, using the opportunity of seeing him shirtless to my advantage. He has a runner's body, toned but not muscular. He wraps the towel around his shoulders, then grabs the other one and opens it up. I realize he wants me to stand up, so I do, and he wraps it around me. I take the corners and pull it tighter, stepping out of the tub onto the deck. The cold wood immediately saps the warmth generated by the hot tub. I quickly dry off and then wrap myself up in the robe.

"I hope you don't mind my borrowing this," I say. "I found it in the closet."

He shrugs. "It's Mac's. I doubt he'd mind."

No wonder it's so big. Lucas opens the door for me, and I follow him up to our room. He grabs a change of clothes. "You take the bathroom down the hall. I'll use the one in the basement."

He leaves, shutting the door behind him. I take off the robe and hang it in the closet, then gather up my pajamas. My skin prickles from the cold, my wet swimsuit not helping. I open the bedroom door, prepared to make a dash for the bathroom, but run into something solid in the hallway.

Warm hands grab my arms and steady me. I raise my head until I meet Mac's blank face, feeling my cheeks burn with embarrassment.

"Sorry about that," I say. "Didn't see you."

He says nothing.

I chuckle nervously. "Though how anyone can miss someone as big as you is a mystery."

His expression doesn't change. "Sorry again," I say, sliding past him and darting into the bathroom.

I take a deep breath, shaking my head as I release it. I take a long, hot shower, hoping Mac will be gone when I get out and I can retreat into my room without further mortification.

Piper: I literally ran into Mac while wearing the red bikini. *red-cheeked face emoji*

Christy: I thought the bikini was for Lucas. *confused face emoji*

Piper: I'd just come from hanging out in the hot tub with Lucas.

Christy: Ooh, hot tubbing together. How was it? Did he appreciate the bikini? *winky face emoji*

Piper: Yes, he did. *grinning face emoji* He also looks good in a swimsuit. *drooling face emoji*

Christy: And his brother was there too? Bet that was awkward. *grimacing face emoji*

Piper: No, it was just me and Lucas. I slammed into Mac in the hallway on my way to the shower. *melting face emoji*

Christy: Shake it off. You went hot tubbing with Lucas! *party horn emoji* *clinking champagne glass emoji*

Chapter Twelve

Mac

I barely slept last night, but it wasn't because there were visions of sugarplums dancing in my head in anticipation of Christmas morning. Nope. My mind spent hours ruminating on a beautiful woman in a red bikini and the too-brief experience of having her pressed against my torso. I could tell she was embarrassed about running into me, and I wanted to say something to reassure her, but she bolted before my brain could come up with anything useful.

So instead I made myself scarce while she was in the bathroom. A small part of me thought really hard about attempting to recreate the earlier run-in, but the rational part of my brain quickly overruled that part by reminding me she's dating my brother. I needed a reality check and used the sobering thought to head down to the living room and work on the puzzle.

But it just wasn't as much fun without someone fitting pieces together with me. Normally, I don't mind puzzling solo. I'm usually the only one who does puzzles when we're all together, but Piper put together half of the candy cane puzzle on her own, and it was mesmerizing to watch. She sees color in a way my eyes don't. While failing to find the right spots for the remaining pieces, I kept one ear on the noises coming from upstairs. When I heard footsteps move swiftly down the hall and a door shutting, I gave it fifteen more minutes before going upstairs to brush my teeth.

The bathroom smelled of vanilla and sugar, almost as if someone had been baking cookies. I peeked in the shower but couldn't find the source. I'm slightly ashamed to say that I rummaged through the toiletries bag she left in the bathroom and found a small bottle of lotion that matched the scent. I may or may not have rubbed some on my arms.

Okay, so that may have been part of the problem with my not being able to sleep. Every time I moved in the bed, the fresh-baked cookie smell hit my nose. And when I managed to push out the image of Piper in her swimsuit, one of her in my robe quickly replaced it. It practically swallowed her, and yet I think she might have looked sexier in that than in the bikini.

I've had that robe since I was in high school. It lives at my parents' house, but I'm tempted to take it with me when I leave. Just because I remember how cozy it is, of course. No other reason.

When it's finally an acceptable time to go downstairs on Christmas morning, I make a beeline for the coffeemaker. Thankfully, Mom has already made a full pot. I pour a cup and then walk over to the sliding glass doors that look out on the mountains. It snowed last night, which makes everything look soft and sleepy. I take a swig from my mug, letting the hot liquid warm me from the inside. If today is like Christmases past, Mom went back to bed after setting up the coffeemaker, and I'll have a quiet house for at least another hour. I grab a sugar cookie from the kitchen, noticing that Piper's winning creation is still in the container, and then sit on the couch. Mom has already turned on the tree lights, and they cast a soft glow across the living room. Presents are nestled under the tree.

I sink into the couch, feeling my eyes drooping. A nap sounds perfect, so I set my mug on the coffee table and stretch out on the couch, pulling a throw blanket down over my torso. My body grows heavy, and I'm almost out when I hear a creak on the stairs. I blink my eyes open. Piper is tiptoeing down the rest of the stairs, her shoulders hiked to her ears.

"I'm awake," I grumble.

She grimaces, her nose scrunching up adorably. "Sorry. I forgot about the loud step."

I sit up, the sight of her chasing away all thoughts of relaxing. She's wearing thick socks with candy canes on them, buffalo plaid flannel pajama pants, a shirt that says, "Why is the carpet all wet, Todd?," and my robe, the belt untied.

"I hope you don't mind me using your robe. It's a little chilly this morning."

I clear my throat. "It's fine. Nice shirt."

She looks down, frowning slightly. "Thanks."

"You want some coffee?"

She perks up. "Coffee sounds amazing."

I jump up off the couch. "Sit. I'll get it."

Instead of settling into a seat, she follows me into the kitchen while I look through our selection of mugs until I find the one I think is perfect for her. "How do you take your coffee?"

"With a little hazelnut creamer if you have some."

I fill the cup two-thirds full of coffee and then open the fridge door, finding the creamer on the top shelf. I begin pouring it into the mug. "Say when."

The liquid is almost to the top when she responds. "When."

I look up to see her grinning at me. She must have noticed my grossed-out expression.

"Don't judge. The creamer is good."

"I'll take your word for it. Think you can avoid spilling it?"

She scoffs. "Ye of little faith. I'm a pro."

I watch as she bends down and sucks the liquid out of the cup until there's no longer a risk of coffee sloshing over the edge. Then, she picks up the cup and turns it so she can see the design. She snorts, which does something weird to my chest. It feels like I've been sucker-punched.

She turns the cup toward me. It's a winter cap with earflaps and Christmas lights strung between the words "You serious, Clark?"

"I take it your family is also a fan of *Christmas Vacation*," she says, gesturing to her shirt.

I nod, wondering if Luc has a shirt that matches Piper's. He rarely gets into the Christmas spirit unless a competition is involved, but people do out-of-character things for people they love, so it's not out of the realm of possibility.

"Tell me what Christmas morning is usually like with your family," Piper says, interrupting my musing.

I'm surprised Luc hasn't already given her the lowdown on what to expect. Though maybe he has, and she's just making conversation.

"Once everyone's up, which is probably in another hour, we empty our stockings while the breakfast casserole and cinnamon rolls cook. After breakfast, we gather around the tree and open gifts. We hang out for most of the day watching movies, playing games, or skiing—whatever people want to do. And then we have an early dinner and go caroling around the neighborhood."

Her eyes widen. "Caroling? Is this something lots of people do or just your family?"

Her reaction makes me wonder if she doesn't like singing in public. It won't really matter because Dad and Uncle John are loud enough to drown out everyone else. "Just us, though sometimes people will join us along the way. Oh, and we also wear ugly Christmas sweaters."

Her forehead scrunches. "Oh, shoot. I have one at home, but didn't bring it with me."

I'm not surprised Luc failed to tell her about our caroling tradition. He isn't very good at anticipating other people's needs and probably didn't think about the fact that she wouldn't know our activity schedule.

"No worries. There are several in the closet upstairs. Wear whichever one you want."

She smiles. "Thanks, Mac."

My chest warms. A guy could get used to that smiling face. Except that guy isn't going to be me. *Get it together, Mac. This is Luc's girlfriend.*

I need to put some distance between us so I can get my head right, but I don't want to be rude. Thankfully, Elise comes up from the basement and joins us in the kitchen. I turn on the oven to let it preheat, guessing that more family members will be awake soon.

She grabs a mug with a picture of the leg lamp from *A Christmas Story* and pours some coffee before dumping in a ton of sugar. I wrinkle my nose in disgust. How can she drink that? Elise asks Piper how she slept, and I use the opportunity to grab my mug from the coffee table and dash upstairs to my room. Safely alone, I spend a good ten minutes reminding myself that Piper is a no-fly zone and I need to do whatever it takes to tamp down the attraction I feel for her.

Once I'm confident my emotions are under control, I head back downstairs to warm up my coffee. I should have done it earlier, but I'd been too distracted. Mom is in the kitchen putting foil over the casserole. She sticks it in the oven with the cinnamon rolls and then encourages everyone to find a seat in the living room. Nana, Uncle John, and Elise take the couch. Dad is on the loveseat with an empty spot for Mom. I grab a chair from the kitchen and set it next to the couch at just the right angle so that I can't see Luc and Piper cuddled up together in the recliner. I'm not jealous or anything, just want a good view of the tree.

Mom hands out stockings, and I notice there's a new one with Piper's name on it. My stomach twists uncomfortably. Okay, maybe I'm a *little* jealous. But I should be happy for my brother. He deserves to find someone well suited to him, and if that's Piper, then good for him.

My mind is super helpful and reminds me of my glance at her phone yesterday. Does Luc know about this Sam guy Piper's been texting? I suppose he could be a friend or Piper's brother. I don't know that much about her. But managing their relationship is not on my task list. My eyes drift over toward the recliner, and I shift forward in my chair. Bad idea. Now I have an unobstructed view of the couple. Piper has unwrapped a chocolate from her stocking and is holding it toward Luc. I frown. Doesn't she know he hates chocolate?

Luc grins at her and leans forward with his mouth open. His lips touch her fingers as she lets go, and then he takes her hand and presses a kiss to the back of it as their eyes connect. I look away, not wanting to see what happens next. I guess I was wrong about his chocolate aversion.

Mom hands me my stocking, and I busy myself with peeking inside. There's a puzzle magazine inside along with a pair of socks with airplanes on them, some chocolates, a pack of gum, an orange, and a new winter hat. I won't need it when I return to South Carolina after the holiday, but I can keep it here for next Christmas. My stomach lurches at the reminder that my family is expecting my return to Steamboat Springs. I know the promise I made before I joined the Air Force, but it seems unreasonable to be held to something I said over a decade ago when I was young and unsure about what I wanted. I love what I do and would love to continue to fly, but the tug of responsibility and doing right by family is weighing heavily on me. I know I can't let my family down. I'm just going to have to find a way to let go of my selfish desire. I won't be like Luc and abandon my responsibility just because I don't feel like it.

"What does your family do on Christmas?" Nana says.

I look up, realizing she's talking to Piper, who looks a little uncomfortable.

"Well, we used to stay awake until midnight on Christmas Eve and then open one present and go to bed. My dad found it helped calm me down enough to fall asleep. Even as adults, we still did it.

And then the next morning, we'd eat breakfast, open the rest of our gifts, and watch a Christmas movie."

Nana smiles. "That sounds lovely. Do you think they're continuing the tradition without you this year?"

Piper ducks her head and takes a deep breath. "Actually, my mom died when I was little, and my dad passed away a few years ago."

My stomach drops. That's terrible. Luc should have told us so we wouldn't bring it up. It's obviously still tender for her, judging by the pained look on her face. Anger wells up inside me at Luc's lack of forethought. Again.

Mom reaches over and grabs Piper's hand. "Oh, I'm so sorry."

Piper gives her a sad smile. "It's actually kind of nice being somewhere different this year. I appreciate you all welcoming me into your family traditions."

"Of course. We're so happy to have you."

"Do you have any siblings?" Elise asks.

Piper shakes her head. "Just me."

Oof. I wonder if our family togetherness and fun actually hurt Piper, and she's just being nice about the situation. Not that I can ask her. That's something she'd discuss with her boyfriend. Who should make sure she's okay. I glare at my oblivious brother, who's digging through his stocking rather than paying attention to the conversation. I grab one of my chocolates and throw it at him. It bounces off the top of his hard head.

"Hey, who did that?" Luc says, looking up.

I turn my head away, pretending to admire the tree. When I look back, Luc's eyes are narrowed suspiciously at me. I shrug my shoulders, hoping he buys my innocent act. It reminds me of the year we got Nerf guns and spent all afternoon sneaking up on one another and shooting when it was least expected. After Luc pelted me in the shower, Mom confiscated the guns for a week. I chuckle at the memory.

"Hey, Luc," I say. "Remember the year of the Nerf guns?"

He laughs, his eyes sparkling. "We had welts for weeks."

Mom groans. "You two were awful to each other. I'm so glad you've grown up."

I don't know about that. We're still pretty competitive with each other. If I could wrestle Luc for Piper, I probably would. Of course, he knows I'd beat him in physical combat, so he'd probably suggest a sprint or something where we're more evenly matched. Scratch that. He'd propose a ski-off. However, as motivated as I'd be to win, it would probably be a photo finish.

The oven timer goes off in the kitchen, interrupting my thoughts.

"All right, gang," Mom says. "Time for breakfast and then presents!"

My eyes wander back over to Luc and Piper. She's switched her candy cane socks for the snowman ones that were in her stocking and is quietly teasing him about something. He shakes his head, but he's smiling. She seems way too good for him. Maybe it's just because she's nothing like the other women he's dated. They were very business-focused, like Luc. At least the ones I heard about from Elise were. None of them were as playful and easygoing as Piper. Of course, if I'm honest, I don't think I've ever met anyone like Piper.

Uncle John grabs my shoulder and squeezes. "Hop to it, Mac, and bring that chair to the table or you'll be standing while you eat."

I grunt in response, but do as I'm told. Throughout breakfast, my gaze keeps wandering over to Luc and Piper. I really hope he got her something amazing for Christmas. After failing to tell us about her family and thus forcing her to endure an awkward conversation, he really needs to step it up and show her how much he appreciates her.

Chapter Thirteen

Piper

I'm pretty quiet during breakfast, listening to Lucas's family talk about memories from years past. There's lots of laughter, and it makes me miss my dad even more. It was always just the two of us as far back as I can remember. While not as rowdy as the Cahill family, our holidays were just as fun. We'd open our gifts and then watch a Christmas movie while eating the candy from our stockings. Later, I'd give him a fashion show of all the clothes I received. Then we'd play some games before sitting down to a lunch of lasagna and garlic bread. Not your traditional holiday spread, but Dad and I would assemble the lasagna the night before, and the memories of our time in the kitchen still give me warm fuzzies. He taught me how to make a lot of family recipes. I haven't made lasagna since he died. I'm not sure if I'll ever resume that tradition. It's still too painful to think about making it alone.

When everyone has had their fill of casserole and ooey-gooey out-of-this-world cinnamon rolls, Susie herds all of us back to the living room for presents. I lead Lucas over to the loveseat as Hank has already claimed the recliner. I wonder where Susie's going to sit, but then Mac brings two chairs in from the kitchen table. I've noticed he always seems very in tune with what the family needs. Is that innate or something he's learned over the years? Lucas doesn't seem to have the same trait. Not that it means he's uncaring. I think part of his obliviousness is his youth. Mac seems quite a bit older than Lucas. If I had to guess, I'm somewhere near the midpoint of their age gap.

Elise is assigned the task of handing out presents. I'm a little nervous about how my gifts will be received. Lucas wasn't much help in giving me ideas of what everyone might like, so I did a little social media stalking before rushing to stores and am hoping for the best. I'm banking on this family being one who believes the thought counts the most. His mom, sister, and grandmother are receiving prints of paintings I made of Colorado landscapes when I was in undergrad. His dad and uncle will get bottles of scotch. I found a smartphone-controlled paper airplane kit that seemed like something fun for a pilot. Though now that I've met Mac and know how serious he is, I wonder if he'll think it's dumb and childish. Well, it's too late now.

I obviously put the most thought into Lucas's gift, trying to hit the tiny target of something a seriousish girlfriend would give the guy she possibly loves that could also be delivered to my apartment three days before Christmas. I managed to find something fun but also useful. I don't know how he'll receive it, but I've got a story to help sell it to the family.

Elise hands me a box addressed to me from Santa. I'm guessing it's from Lucas's mom based on the neat cursive handwriting.

Inside is a beautifully painted clay bowl. When I turn it over, the artist's name is engraved on the bottom. I make a note to look them up later. I watch the rest of the family tear into gifts. This family is not a one-present-at-a-time group. It's everyone for themselves, so I almost miss when Lucas opens his gift from me. He looks puzzled as he pulls the pen stand out of the box.

"What's that?" Nana asks, pointing at Lucas.

He turns it around so everyone can see the knight holding a giant sword and guarding a fountain pen. I snuggle up against Lucas.

"I thought Lucas needed a nice pen for when he signs all of his amazing deals with clients. Plus, it reminded me of the time he rescued me outside of our office. It was raining, and I'd forgotten my umbrella, so I was rushing to the front doors. I wasn't watching where I was going, and my heel slid right into the storm drain grate and wouldn't come out. Out of nowhere, there he was with an umbrella that he handed to me while unsticking my shoe. Thanks to him, my shoe was saved, and I only looked like a half-drowned rat. He was my knight in shining armor that day."

"Aww," Susie says, clasping her hands to her chest. "What a sweet story."

"Thanks, Pipes," Lucas says, kissing my cheek. He leans in closer and whispers. "I don't remember that happening."

I move my mouth to his ear. "Because it didn't," I whisper back.

He grins over at me, then wraps me in a hug. "I really like the pen holder. You're the best," he says, forgetting to whisper.

I feel the compliment zing through my body. Perhaps my plan is working, and he has a glimpse of how good we could be together.

"What did Luc get you?" Elise asks.

Lucas looks like a prisoner being spotlighted during an escape attempt. I guess that means he didn't get me anything. There's a twinge of disappointment, but we're not actually dating. Still, this entire scheme was his idea, so he should have considered that I'd need a gift from my boyfriend. I'm curious to see how he handles things. He always seems cool under pressure at work. Is he the same when he's around his family?

He turns to me, taking my hands in his. "I had something custom-made for you, but unfortunately it wasn't ready before we left. I'm sorry I can't give it to you now."

"Describe it to her."

Lucas narrows his eyes at his sister, clearly unamused by her pestering. Still, other than his initial reaction, he appears in control.

"If you must know, it's a photo book of our time together with little snippets of my favorite memories."

My heart flips. That would be a pretty awesome gift. But, since I know we have no memories together before this week, it's just confirmation that giving me a Christmas present never crossed his mind. I'm sure that if we were really together, he'd be much more considerate, but a small part of me is doubtful. Have I built up a fake version of Lucas in my mind?

I remember I'm supposed to be reacting to what Lucas just said, so I wrap my arms around his neck and hug him tight. After a few seconds, I feel one of his arms around my waist.

"That's so great! I can't wait to see it." I lean into him so I can whisper in his ear. "Great save. You're quick on your feet."

He chuckles. "Thanks for playing along. We make a great team."

Does he really consider us a team? I mean, that's sort of what we are. It would be nice if I knew there was a real chance for us to be more than co-conspirators. Right now I feel like my emotions are all over the place. I came on this trip to show Lucas we'd make a good match, but so far there's been conflicting evidence that's true. He's more hot and cold with his attention than I like in a relationship. I definitely prefer someone who is consistent and attentive. The surprise of his handsome brother has thrown me off guard as well. It's certainly more than a little inconvenient to be attracted to two brothers at the same time. Maybe while I'm playing the part of Lucas's girlfriend, I should also figure out if that's really what I want. Yes, he's attractive and charismatic, but a loving and secure relationship cannot be built only on superficial qualities.

Piper: Merry Christmas! Get anything good?

Christy: Brooks booked us an all-inclusive in St. Lucia! *sun emoji* *beach umbrella emoji*

Piper: Fancy! *sunglasses face emoji* I hope it's soon so you can get out of the cold weather.

Christy: It's in February. Did Lucas get you anything? A kiss maybe? *winky face* *kissy face*

Piper: No, unfortunately, but his mom got me a beautiful bowl. *present emoji*

Christy: *disappointed face emoji*

Chapter Fourteen

Mac

I'm livid Luc doesn't have a present for his girlfriend. Even if he's having a photo book made, which I'm skeptical about, he could still have also gotten a little something for Piper to open. It's what I would have done. Instead, she has a bowl Mom gave her, and that's it. I really should have picked something up for her, but I thought it might be awkward for her to receive something from the brother of her boyfriend, who she's never met. Now I think it would have been better to have risked that awkwardness over this current one of practically excluding her from the gift exchange.

Especially since she brought a gift for everyone in our family. She obviously did some homework because Dad and Uncle John have already opened their bottles, while Mom, Nana, and Elise are delighted by their art pieces. Even I was touched by the thoughtfulness of Piper's gift for Luc. She truly sees my brother and understands his focus on work and his desire to be seen as a hero.

There's a gift bag at my feet I have yet to open. It's from Piper, and while I'm very curious to see what it is, my stomach twists uncomfortably at the fact that I have nothing to give in return. I should have listened to my instinct and gotten her a candle or something. It would have been generic, but probably so is what's in this bag, seeing as how she doesn't know me at all. I pull out the sparkly white paper and look inside. There's a box with a picture of a paper airplane. It's a little balsam flyer kit.

I pull it out of the bag and read the box, realizing I was wrong. It's a smartphone-controlled paper airplane. I'm supposed to make the basic structure out of sturdy paper and then attach the nose and propellers and fly it using an app. I've never seen one of these before and want to see how well it flies. I haven't played with toys in forever, but feel like I'm ten years old again and just received my first RC car.

When I glance over at Piper, she's looking at me. I hold up the box and mouth a thank you. She nods, giving me a half-smile, like she's concerned I don't like it. I force myself to smile. Her forehead crinkles, making me wonder if it looks more like a grimace. I will thank her properly later. In the meantime, I want to get everything set up so I can mess around with it. The motorized part needs to charge, so I plug it in and take the rest of the kit to the kitchen table to make the body of the plane.

Satisfied with my design, I look up and realize the rest of the family is still in the living room opening gifts. Oops. I go back to the living room after checking the battery on the plane nose. It still needs fifteen minutes before it'll be fully charged. Surely we'll be done with gifts by then.

When the tree skirt is barren, I grab a garbage bag and clean up the trash, then return to the kitchen to assemble the plane. I put on a coat and hat, stuff my feet into a pair of boots, and carry my plane out to the driveway. When everything is set up on my phone, I pull my arm back and then shoot it forward, releasing the plane. It arcs across the road, and I use the app to keep it flying. I'm giddy with excitement. This is more fun than I thought it'd be. I hear a door open and close behind me, but I keep my eyes on the plane so it doesn't end up in a tree.

I have no idea how much time has passed before my phone lights up with a low-power warning for the plane's motor. It feels like only five minutes, but I bet it's been much longer. I turn the plane around so it's headed back toward me. I forgot to check whether I'm supposed to catch it or let it land. With snow everywhere, I don't think it's a good idea for the paper wings to hit the ground, so I decide to catch it. It's coming in faster than I expected, so I aim it for my chest, trusting my coat to act as a cushion. When it hits me, I drop both arms underneath to cradle it.

"Impressive."

I turn around. Piper is smiling at me. My heart thumps against my chest in response. I'd just assumed it was Mom. If I'd known it was Piper…I wouldn't have done anything different other than feel silly for acting like a teenage boy with my new toy.

"Thanks. It's really cool."

"I'm glad you like it. I was a little worried you'd think it was immature, but I thought it looked really neat, and you're a pilot, so…" She shrugs.

My chest warms. Piper's so thoughtful. What in the world does she see in my brother?

"It's great. I haven't gotten anything this cool since I was a kid. It makes me feel young again."

She scoffs. "You sound like an old man. You're what, in your thirties?"

"Thirty-four."

She's five years older than Luc but seems decades more mature. Of course, maybe I'm still seeing the old Luc. He could have grown up a lot in the last few years. It's not like we see each other often enough to really get a good feel for one another.

"I'm sorry I didn't get you a gift."

She waves away my apology. "I know I overdid it getting everyone a present even though I'd never met you, but I wanted to make a good impression." Her face gives away her embarrassment. "I hope that doesn't sound self-serving."

"Of course not."

"Good. I was sent out here to tell you your mom wants your help with dinner."

"Thanks. Hey, grab whichever sweater you want for tonight, and I'd suggest lots of layers. It's usually pretty chilly."

Her brow furrows adorably before clearing again. "Right, caroling. Will there be songbooks or...?"

I shake my head. "We sing the classics, so you should know the words. And if not, it's okay to make them up. That's what Dad and Uncle John do."

She grins. "So no pressure then."

Piper turns and heads back into the house. I follow, dropping my new gift off in my room and closing the door. If I leave it out, someone might mess with it, and I don't want to risk Piper's gift to me getting broken.

Most of the afternoon is taken up with dinner prep. Mom gives everyone a task. I work at the island peeling potatoes next to Piper, who has salad duty. Luc is noticeably absent, which means I also end up in charge of the broccoli casserole. He's probably doing work. I don't think he knows the true meaning of a vacation. While I'm perturbed on Piper's behalf, I'm also secretly happy for the opportunity to spend more time with her. We discuss our favorite foods and desserts while we work. I learn about her family tradition of eating lasagna on Christmas and consuming twelve grapes at midnight on New Year's Eve for good fortune and prosperity. She and her dad started eating grapes when they lived in Spain.

I can tell it's hard for her to talk about her father. I'd like to know more, but I don't want to pry. Maybe I'll ask Luc what the story is there. Assuming he was listening when she told him.

Luc shows up in the kitchen when Mom calls everyone for dinner. He's in his ugly Christmas sweater already. I dash upstairs to grab mine and select one for Piper as well. The one I usually wear has trees, snowflakes, and ornaments with a couple of rows of airplanes knitted in among everything else. Mom gave it to me the year I earned my pilot's license.

Back downstairs, I hand the other one to Piper. She seems to notice for the first time that everyone is already wearing theirs and quickly puts it on. It's a red, white, and green Fair Isle pattern with alternating rows of Santa faces and reindeer. It engulfs her so much she rolls up the sleeves a few times. The bottom hits mid-thigh and looks more like a dress than a top. She looks so cute. I turn away before anyone notices me staring and head to the kitchen to see if Mom needs help carrying food in.

Dinner is a raucous affair as everyone makes fun of everyone else's sweater choice. Luc's is burgundy and white with big fir trees and moose on it. Elise's green sweater with big white buttons makes her look like an elf. Dad's has horizontal stripes of various colors and thickness and must be forty years old because it's in every family holiday photo I've ever seen. Mom and Uncle John have more understated sweaters in solid colors with patterns only around the neck, but Nana's depicts Santa and his elves preparing for Christmas.

"So, Piper," Nana says. "Do you have any friends you could set Mac up with?"

I choke on the bite of food I just took, and Elise smacks me hard on the back.

Piper looks over at me. "I don't really know his type."

I look down at my plate. "Blondes. Tall ones."

"My only blonde friend is already married, unfortunately."

I feel Elise's eyes on me. "You like brunettes," she says.

I make the mistake of glancing over at Piper because her eyes widen in surprise when our gazes catch. I clear my throat and stuff a forkful of food into my mouth so I don't have to answer.

Luckily, Uncle John and Dad start arguing loudly about which song we should sing first, which draws everyone's attention.

"'Deck the Halls' is a classic," Dad says.

"And yet you still manage to mangle the words," Uncle John says. "'We Wish You a Merry Christmas' is nearly impossible to mess up."

"No one cares about the words as long as you sing the right melody with gusto."

"I think people notice when you sing about a troll in a Christmas carol."

Dad harrumphs. "Mom, you pick the first song."

Nana looks up. "What was that?"

"What song should we sing first?" Uncle John asks.

"'We Wish You a Merry Christmas', of course."

Uncle John grins, raising his fists in the air. Dad sighs, shakes his head, and grabs a yeast roll.

When dinner is over, we all bundle up and head outside. Mom marches us down to the end of the block and knocks on the first door. When it opens, we launch into the first song. I chuckle when I hear Uncle John mumble the third verse. So much for knowing all the words. We sing two more songs before heading to the next house. The young couple who open the door look a little bewildered at first, but join us when we tell them what we're doing.

At the third house, I find myself standing next to Piper and am surprised when her clear soprano voice rings out as we sing "Angels We Have Heard on High." She's beautiful, can sing, and gives great gifts? The more I learn about her, the more I like. I'm going to have to stamp out this infatuation before I cross a line. Tomorrow I'll go skiing with Elise or find something else that gets me out of Piper's orbit. It's probably just all this close proximity that has me thinking improper thoughts.

An hour later we're at the last house, the one right next to ours. It belongs to the Little family. We used to see them every Christmas, but not since they decided to spend holidays in Europe and turned it into a rental. So it's a surprise when the door opens and I recognize the blonde woman who emerges.

"Darcy!" Mom says, walking up the steps to hug her. "What are you doing here?"

"So great to see the Cahill family," she says, her eyes passing over us.

Is it just me, or did she pause on Luc's face for a few beats longer than everyone else's?

"I missed the mountain, so I told my dad I wanted to come here for Christmas. They still wanted to go to Switzerland, so it's just me."

"Oh, sweetheart," Mom says. "You should have told us you were here. You must come over for dinner tomorrow night. And you can go skiing with the kids during the day. It'll be just like old times!"

"I'd love to, thanks."

"Actually," Luc says, "I have to go to Denver tomorrow, but I'm sure Elise and Mac would be happy to ski with you."

"Oh, Luc," Mom says, disappointment in her voice. "Are you really working the day after Christmas?"

"It's a big client, Mom. I'll be back in time for dinner, I promise."

"What about Piper?" Nana says, echoing my thoughts.

"I'll be fine," Piper says. "I've been wanting to explore the town, so I can do that while everyone else skis."

I don't like the idea of her being in town all alone. "Elise and Darcy can go skiing. I'll go to town with Piper."

Luc gives me an appreciative smile. "Great, it's settled."

I scowl back because I can't believe he's putting work over his relationship. One day that's going to burn him. He really needs to get his priorities straight. I should have a talk with him. But first, I have to contend with the fact that I agreed to spend more time with Piper after I'd just decided I needed space from her. I'm shooting myself in the foot, but I can't stand by and let her fend for herself. It's not what she signed up for when she agreed to come with Luc on a family holiday. The least I can do is make sure she feels welcome and has fun. It's the right thing to do, even if it makes my chest feel tight.

Chapter Fifteen

Piper

The next morning, Mac and I sit quietly next to each other on the ride into town. Across the row from us, Elise and Darcy are chatting away like best friends. I'm a little jealous of their closeness. I'd love to have someone who has known me through various ages and stages of life. My dad and I were somewhat nomadic. Since he was a photographer, he went where the work was, which meant living all over the world. Not that I don't appreciate the experiences I've had, but there's just something inviting about having roots somewhere and frequently running into people who know you. Of course, since I have no idea what that's like, perhaps it isn't as amazing as it sounds, but I feel strongly that being known by some is better than not being known by anyone. Sure, I've got Christy, but one person can't meet all my relational needs. Perhaps making more connections should be part of my goals for the new year.

Lucas told me about Darcy when we were in our room last night. The families have known each other for twenty years. Lucas and Darcy went to school together and had many classes together, since they were in the same year. She went to college out of state, so they only saw her at Christmas and in the summers until graduation, and then haven't seen her since. I'd noticed Darcy stealing glances at Lucas from her front porch when we stopped to sing, and I've been wondering if they have a more intimate past than just being neighbors and classmates. Something stopped me from asking outright. Probably because I don't want him to see me as the jealous type. However, I also noticed Lucas's eyes taking in Darcy when she opened the door, and the appreciation in his eyes showed me I still have a lot of work to do if I want him to see I'm the perfect woman for him. Emphasis on "if" because this trip has shown me I really don't know a lot about Lucas, and what I've learned thus far makes me question our compatibility.

I reaffirmed my amiability about the whole "Lucas working over the holiday" situation, even praising him for being so passionate about his work. Unlike his family, who grumbled all the way home about Lucas taking off to Denver for work today. I think my unwavering support raised me a little higher in his estimation. He made a show of giving me a big hug and kissing my cheek in front of his family before he headed to the airport. Still no actual kiss, though I'm not going to initiate it. As much as I'd like him to pick me, I have enough pride not to force anything. I'm not that desperate, though I am definitely falling in love with his family.

Lucas's parents have been so gracious. His mom gushed about her Christmas gift from me, and Hank was impressed I found his favorite scotch. Nana Cahill is so sweet, patting my hands and giving my arms warm presses whenever we cross paths. My heart squeezes with longing for my own close-knit family every time. Celebrating Christmas with a family that includes both parents, siblings, and extended family shows me what I was missing all these years. It's going to be really hard to let everyone go after the holiday. It's a powerful incentive for me to show Lucas why we should be together for real.

Of course, that's really hard to do without actually spending time with Lucas. I can see why his last girlfriend broke up with him. She probably didn't feel like a priority to him, and possibly a little lonely, which shouldn't happen when you're in a relationship. You should feel seen, wanted, and cherished. At least, that's what I think.

The shuttle stops at the mountain base area, and we get off. Mac guides me over to another shuttle that will take us into downtown. When we disembark, I glance up at Mac, startled at how tall he looks today. In the house, he doesn't seem so large, but perhaps it's because he's sitting most of the time.

"Where should we go first?"

He glances around. "It depends on what you're looking for. There's a bookstore, clothing shops, gifts, groceries, coffee, chocolate, candy..."

Duh. All the usual places. "How about the best place to find something for tonight's White Elephant Exchange? And also, maybe an insider's knowledge of what is historically gifted at this party. Is it useless stuff or semi-nice but impersonal things like gift cards and bottles of wine?"

One corner of his mouth tips up for a second before returning to its usual flat line. It's really hard to believe our first encounter, when he was flirting and super smiley, actually happened. He's like a completely different person around his family. What's that about? Maybe his playfulness was the anomaly. It's just the two of us today, so we'll see.

"It's a hodgepodge of stuff. The older people usually put in alcohol, while the younger folks are wild cards. In the past, there have been candy, chocolate, board games, and items with jokes or puns on them. One year, Uncle John wrapped up a roll of paper towels but had stuffed money down the paper tube and didn't tell anyone until the game was over. Elise was ecstatic, and we all wished we'd stolen it from her."

I like John's sneakiness. It's what I've done in past exchanges.

"That helps a lot. Have you gotten your gift already?"

"No, but I know what I'm doing. How do you feel about visiting a thrift store?"

I smile. "I love thrift stores! You never know what you're going to find. Let's do it."

Mac points down the street, and we start walking. I spend most of the short trek with my head on a swivel, taking in all the store-fronts on either side of the street. I'm just as enamored with the Old West feel as I was a few days ago. It invites me to slow down and savor each moment. I wonder what it'd be like to live here.

"Did you like growing up here?"

I feel Mac's eyes on me, but I'm too busy taking in the beautiful scenery.

"It's a great place for someone who loves the outdoors. Lots of hiking year-round, skiing in the winter, boating, mountain biking, and fishing in the summers. I practically lived in a tent every summer."

From the fondness in his voice, I can tell he had a good childhood. I wonder why he moved away. Probably because he had to go where the Air Force sent him. Though from a few conversations this week, it sounds like he might move back soon. Dare I pry? I dare.

"Pardon me if I'm being a Nosy Nellie, but it sounds like you might be returning to Steamboat Springs to work at the resort. Do I have that right?"

"Yes."

His clipped response is a startling contrast to his previous gushing about the town. It appears I've stumbled upon a sore spot. Now I'm really curious, but our time in town is just beginning, and I don't want to spend the rest of my day with a walking stone statue, so I think of something to turn the conversation. Thankfully, we've reached the store, and a creature on the wall just inside the door steals my attention. I yank open the door and walk toward the surprising sight, needing a closer look.

"That would be a first for the exchange. How would you wrap it?"

I feel Mac behind me but don't turn, still stunned by the taxidermied mountain lion perched on a log. "My thoughts were actually about whether I could take that on the plane home."

There's a rumble of a laugh near my ear, and I turn just in time to see a small smile on Mac's face before his serious face returns. There's a divot between his eyebrows like he's thinking about my conundrum.

"Your best bet would probably be to ship it. That way you can secure it with bubble wrap."

Oh, he thinks I'm serious. I step closer, searching for a price tag. My eyes bulge when I see it's two hundred dollars.

"Unfortunately, it's a bit rich for my blood and out of the exchange price limit. Besides, it'd probably scare Maui."

"Who's Maui?"

"My cat."

"You're probably right. I'm going to search for a gift. Let me know when you're ready to go, but take your time, yeah?"

I tear my eyes from the stuffed cat and turn to face Mac. "Sure."

He disappears through a doorway to the right. It's filled with books, which are always a point of interest for me. I'll look through it later after Mac vacates the room. I pass by a bunch of stereo equipment followed by a row of horse saddles. There's a rotary telephone and a non-working typewriter.

Nothing looks like a winner, so I wander over to the clothing section. There's an entire rack of Christmas shirts, and I browse through them, chuckling at one with two light bulbs having a conversation. One says, "Working over the holidays?" and the other responds. "Yes, off and on." It makes me think of Lucas, and I decide I don't want to bring up that reminder in front of the rest of the family, so I keep looking.

I wind up in a miscellaneous aisle, and my eyes catch on a neon pink photo album with black hearts all over it. Picking it up, I leaf through the pages. Someone donated it with photos still in it. This feels like something I'd normally get for a White Elephant exchange, but what could I do with it to make it a sneakily worthwhile gift? While I think over the possibilities, I carry it around with me. The answer comes to me as I'm browsing the titles in the book room and spot *Think and Grow Rich* on the shelf. My smile curls up like the Grinch when he decides to steal Christmas from the Whos.

Looking around for Mac, I see him in the back corner. Moving quickly, I pay for my purchase, asking the clerk to wrap it in paper. Then I head back to Mac, who has already purchased his item. The wrapped item is rectangular and similar in size to my purchase.

"You good?" he says when he sees me.

"Yep. But I need to visit a convenience store while we're here."

"No problem. Let's stop there next so we don't forget."

Mac politely waits on the sidewalk at the oddly named Space Station while I dash inside for my purchase. Satisfied I'm ready for the exchange, I take a deep breath, ready to enjoy the rest of our time in town. Not needing anything else in particular, Mac suggests we walk along Lincoln Avenue and visit whatever piques our interest.

"What's SAM?" I ask, pointing across the street at the lit-up window.

"The art museum."

"Ooh, can we go in?"

He shrugs. "Sure."

I'm giddy as we cross the street, anticipating the exhibits we'll find inside. I love being inspired by other artists. I wonder if all the pieces will be made by local artists. We pay the admission and grab a brochure listing the rooms and their contents. There's a western room, a contemporary room, and a special exhibit. The first room has paintings of cowboys riding horses at a rodeo. Hanging from the ceiling is a metal sculpture of a person who appears to be swimming. Not sure what it has to do with the cowboys, but it's interesting to look at. There are also smaller sculptures of cowboys in various action poses—one with a lasso, another in the process of tying up a calf, and a third that appears to be in an all-out sprint. I wonder if he's running from a bull that's thrown him. I enjoy pieces that make me think and imagine. The special exhibit is paintings of the Yampa Valley. They are beautiful depictions of the river, mountains, and trees. Some are so detailed they could be mistaken for photographs. The paintings are for sale, but out of my price range. Still, I spend a long time in front of a painting of the river with trace amounts of snow on the mountains and large cloud shadows darkening the mountainside.

"This place sure is beautiful in the summer, huh?"

Mac's words startle me out of my trance.

"What? Oh, yes. It looks too pretty to be real."

"If it were summer, I could take you to this exact spot. Right now, it's mostly snow, which is also pretty, but there's just something awe-inspiring about the different hues of the rocks."

The warmth from earlier is back in his voice. He definitely cares about this place, even if something has soured him a bit. Unsure of how to respond, I smile and walk into the adjoining room. Its collection comprises photographs of Colorado landmarks: Broncos stadium, Pikes Peak, Red Rocks Amphitheater, lakes, rivers, and a variety of rock formations and historic buildings I don't recognize. We make our way around the room. I read each plaque about the location and artist. One photo farther down the wall catches my eye with its familiarity. It's a photo of clear blue-green water with water cascading off a rock in the background. When I see the name on the plaque, my breath catches and I feel my eyes filling with tears.

"Are you okay?"

There's a light touch on my shoulder. Mac must see the anguish on my face because in a blink his arms are around me and my face is buried in his chest. The surprise gives way to a warm comfort, and I lean into the hug, trying to wipe my eyes furtively while simultaneously taking deep breaths to figure out what he smells like. It's vaguely woodsy but with something kind of smoky mixed in. It's distracting in a good way, and I focus on trying to pinpoint the scents. When I feel like my emotions are under control again, I pull back. Mac's arms drop to his sides, and he shoves his hands into his pants pockets. His lined forehead reveals his concern.

"Sorry about that," I say, feeling sheepish.

"Do we need to leave?"

"No, I'm fine. Just a little surprise grief. It happens sometimes."

"Why does Hanging Lake make you sad? I've always thought it was quite beautiful."

I wave my hand. "It is beautiful. It's not the lake; it's the photo."

At his perplexed expression, I continue.

"My father took that picture."

"He did?" Mac bends down for a closer look before straightening up and turning back to me. "He was very good."

I turn back to the photo. "He was. A great dad, too."

"How did he die?" He winces. "Sorry. Don't answer that. I'm being insensitive."

"No, it's okay. Someone blew through a stop sign and smashed into his car. He was on his way home from dropping me off at the airport. I'd come home for Christmas and was already in the air when the hospital called, so I didn't get the message until I landed in Iceland. I spent a long night waiting for a flight that would take me back to Denver."

"I'm so sorry, Piper."

I give him a small smile. "Thanks."

I'm not sure where to take the conversation, my mind full of memories of the past. Fortunately, Mac comes up with something. Unfortunately, it does nothing to quell the melancholy in my heart.

"So, you're obviously a bit of an artist yourself," he says. "Is that how you ended up in graphic design?"

"Sort of."

I feel like I should explain, but a sudden swell of pain renders me mute. There's no way Mac knows that giving up painting has been one of my biggest regrets. Maybe I should have really gone for making a living with my art, but when Dad died so suddenly, I felt lost and alone and went in search of some security. I found solid ground in a full-time job at Elite Creative. Having somewhere I needed to be on weekdays felt like a lifeline, keeping me from following over the brink into an endless sea of sorrow. I know Dad would have preferred me to go for my dream, but without his unwavering support, I just couldn't do it. Mac puts a hand on my shoulder in an act of comfort, and it takes nearly everything in me not to burst into tears.

"Do you want to get out of here? Maybe get some lunch?"

That's just what I need. How did he know? I nod and clear my throat, hoping my voice won't betray the emotions swirling inside me. "Yeah, that sounds good. Let's go somewhere you like."

We end up at Yampa River Icehouse, where I order a barbecue sandwich and fries. Right after our server leaves, a man approaches our table.

"Bronc? I thought that was you. What are you doing here?"

Mac gets up from his chair and thumps the guy on the back.

"Hey, Twigs. I'm visiting the family for Christmas. What about you?"

He motions to a table on the other side of the room where a smiling woman with blonde curly hair sits. "Maggie wanted to come skiing, and I remember you talking about how great the powder is up here. I forgot you were from here." He glances over at me. "Bronc, you didn't tell me you had a girlfriend." He extends his hand. "Hi, I'm Joe, but friends call me Twigs."

I reach out and shake it. "Piper. No nickname."

Joe laughs. "Ooh, I like her. So, Bronc, you still a CO at Shaw?"

"Yep, I've been teaching night operations recently. I doubt you're still at Kunsan."

"No, I'm at Holloman now, whipping cadets into shape. Who'd have thought we'd ever be training pilots?"

Mac gets a roguish grin on his face that lights him up from the inside. My eyes widen as I get another glimpse of the man I met at the grocery store.

"I know, man. Especially after the stuff we pulled at school. If our CO knew even a quarter of it, we'd have been sent packing for sure."

Twigs laughs. "You know I'll never tell."

"Me neither."

The two continue to chat, throwing out technical terms and acronyms I'll never understand. At one point, they're both bent over laughing about something. I like seeing this playful, carefree side of Mac. Why isn't he always like this? Is it something about his family situation that makes him grumpy? There's definitely some tension between him and Lucas. I haven't missed the narrow-eyed looks he slings Lucas's way. But there's also something sensitive involving his parents. It could just be that they don't see each other very often and so there's a bit of an adjustment when they spend a lot of time together. Not that any of this is my concern, but I can't help noticing that Mac has seemed like two different people to me.

Joe turns to me, smiling. "Sorry we cut you out of the conversation, Piper. That was rude of us."

I shrug. "It's fine. I'm glad you saw us and came over."

He places a hand on Mac's shoulder. "I want you to know Bronc here is the best pilot I ever had the honor of flying with. He's also a good man. Loyal, fearless, smart, and resourceful. You won't find one better."

I'm not really sure what to say to that. I wait for Mac to correct his friend about our situation, but he's silent. His back is to me now, so I can't even tell what his face looks like. Joe's eyes bounce between me and Mac.

"Anyway," Joe says, "I better get back to Mags. Again, nice to meet you, Piper. Be sure to keep my boy here in check. And don't forget to send me an invitation to the wedding."

Whatever look is on Mac's face makes Joe chuckle. He smacks Mac on the shoulder, leans in and whispers something, then heads back to his table. Mac turns and sits down, a troubled look on his face.

"What was that all about, *Bronc*?"

He frowns. "Twigs and I were in the same training class. Everyone eventually receives a nickname. Mine is Bronc."

I lean back in my seat and cross my arms. "I've got to hear this story."

"It's not very exciting. Early in my training, I was struggling to keep the plane steady while refueling in the air and someone said my plane looked like a bucking bronco."

"That sounds kind of scary. Is it hard to refuel while flying?"

"Not if you know what you're doing."

"How did Joe become Twigs?"

He smiles slightly. "He had really skinny legs. Someone said it looked like he was walking on two sticks, and it sort of morphed from there."

I shake my head. "Guys are mean."

He shrugs. "It's a rite of passage and bonds us together."

I lean forward. "So what would my nickname be?"

His eyes widen. "Um...it's really only a thing for cadets."

Is he deflecting the question? I slump back in my chair.

"Never mind, then."

Our food arrives, and I take a huge bite of my sandwich to distract myself from the twinge of disappointment in my gut. I really thought after seeing Mac open up with Joe that we'd be able to maintain that happy, carefree atmosphere. But he reverted to his closed-off self as soon as Joe left. I don't know why it even matters. I'm supposed to be winning Lucas over, not Mac. I turn my thoughts over toward figuring out my plan of action for when he returns from Denver. Unfortunately, I'm drawing a blank.

Chapter Sixteen

Mac

I'm kicking myself for not playing along with Piper and coming up with a nickname for her. But the first one that popped into my head was "Sexy," and that's not appropriate for my brother's girlfriend. It was probably foremost in my mind because I was still dwelling on the experience of feeling her snuggled up against my chest in the art museum. I got another whiff of her shampoo, and it took every ounce of my willpower not to bury my nose in her hair. I feel terrible she was crying, though intellectually I know it wasn't my fault. Still, I'm a protector, and as such I never want people I care about to suffer.

Sure, I've only known Piper a couple of days, but she fits so well into our family that it seems like she's always belonged with us. Maybe that's what Luc sees in her. She has a fun, playful side that probably helps him remember there's more to life than his career. Not that he's shown much clarity on that point, as evidenced by his disappearance this morning. I'm still annoyed at him for choosing work over his family, and especially over Piper. If she were my girlfriend, I'd move heaven and earth to make sure she knew how important she was to me. Of course, I'd do that for any woman I was dating, not only Piper. I'm just saying that people are more important than anything else.

Which is why I'm struggling so much with my lack of desire to join the family business. Intellectually, I know it's the right thing to do, but my heart beats for flying. I know I can't do both the Air Force and the resort and I feel obligated to follow through on my family's plans for me, but it's a challenge when I know there will be resentment on my part for having to give up what I love for what I'm supposed to do. Being back here has ratcheted up the tension I feel. My parents have always been supportive of me, and I know they love me unconditionally, so I feel like it's not too much to ask that their firstborn adhere to their wishes. I just have to get over myself, I guess.

Realizing I'm stuck in my head on our ride back to the house, I search for something to say.

"What did you think of downtown?"

Piper is looking out the window but turns toward me to answer. The sadness on her face is a punch to my gut. I did this. I'm responsible for leaching out her joy.

"It was cute. I may have to return to the bookstore before I leave."

We wandered through it after lunch and then visited a store filled with Steamboat Springs-branded merchandise. Piper picked up a hat for a friend of hers. I wonder if it's that Sam guy she texts with. Her response reminds me of something I wanted to ask her.

"Earlier you said you used to paint. How did you get into it, and why did you stop?"

Her shoulders hunch up to her ears. The silence between us lasts so long, I'm worried I've hit a tripwire. Her hands are clasped so tightly together in her lap that her knuckles are turning white. I'm not sure what has her so distressed, but I feel a compulsion to make it better, so I backtrack just as she finally speaks.

"Never mind. Don't answer that."

She finally looks up at me, and my heart twists when I see the sheen of tears in her eyes.

"When I was a kid, my dad got me a basic art set. I thought his photographs were so beautiful, I tried to capture their essence with my paints. They were terrible, of course, but Dad encouraged me to keep trying. He would hang some of my paintings up around the house to show that he loved them. He even signed me up for painting classes."

She blinks and wipes her eyes.

"He sounds like a great dad."

She tries to smile, but it disappears quickly.

"He pushed me to keep following my passion, even when that meant going to college on the East Coast and then grad school in Europe."

Whoa. She went to grad school for painting? No wonder she killed it in the cookie decorating competition. I wonder what she'd do with an actual canvas and some paints. The answer as to why she's not currently painting is now crystal clear. I ask my question as gently as possible.

"Does painting make you think of your dad?"

She nods, her eyes downcast.

"I know he'd want me to get back to it, but it seems impossible. I'd have to go to New York or somewhere for a real chance to make it in the art world, but my dad loved Colorado, and I feel closer to him here. He grew up near Denver, and there's a small permanent exhibit of his photos in the museum there. Whenever I'm having a tough day, I go look at them, and it almost feels like he's here with me."

My arms ache to draw her close and offer her physical comfort, but it doesn't feel like my place.

"I'm so sorry, Piper."

"It's not your fault."

We reach our stop, but I'm not ready to end this conversation, which I know will happen if we head straight to the house.

"Would you like to take a walk? There's a wooded trail nearby I visit sometimes when I need to clear my head."

"That sounds nice."

Once we're ensconced among the snow-laden trees, the tension in my chest eases. I feel an urge to be vulnerable with her after what she's shared. I take a deep breath and blurt it out.

"My parents want me to take over running the resort, but I'm really struggling because I love flying and don't want to give it up. I know it's selfish, but I can't convince myself to commit to the family business."

"What do you love about flying?"

That's not what I expected her to say, but I'm relieved she's asked a question I have no difficulty answering.

"What don't I love about it? The thrill of zooming through the skies at over five hundred miles an hour. Doing barrel rolls and vertical climbs. Being in formation with other fighters and working through various tactical maneuvers. The satisfaction of hitting a target with precision. The bird's-eye view of the earth from so far up. It's incredible."

When I glance over at her, she's got a delighted smile on her face. "What?"

She shakes her head. "You should see your face. The joy just radiates off of you."

I realize how big my smile is and try to tamp it down. She lightly smacks my coat sleeve.

"Don't do that. It's okay to be excited about something you love."

"I feel bad that I don't feel the same way about the business."

"You shouldn't. I don't know your parents very well, but I bet they'd rather you be happy in your career than fulfill a role purely out of obligation. They seem reasonable. Have you talked to them?"

What she's saying sounds logical, but I know when it comes to family, sometimes emotions win out over a convincing argument. It's one reason Luc skipped Christmas two years ago. He didn't want to deal with our parents' disappointment that he was changing the original plan of all the kids joining the family business by striking out on his own. We can't both follow our hearts. Someone has to step up and keep the legacy going.

"No, because I already know what they'll say. They need me to follow through on the plan, and that's what I'll do. Family first."

Her lips press together like she wants to argue but is doing her best to keep her thoughts to herself. We walk in silence for a minute.

"I still think you should have the conversation. They might surprise you."

I highly doubt it but keep that thought to myself. Instead, I change the topic back to Piper.

"If you went to school for painting, how did you end up as a graphic designer? Wouldn't that require a different education?"

"You're very astute, Mr. Fighter Pilot. I double-majored in fine arts and graphic design. I knew from watching my father that an artist needs to be versatile. I figured if I knew the ins and outs of making art on computers, I'd always be able to find work."

"Is it as fun and fulfilling as I assume painting was?"

She gives me a look I interpret as asking me if I'm crazy.

"I spend my days sitting in a cubicle, staring at a screen, creating images for exciting things like olive oil and tires. What do you think?"

"What would your life look like if you were painting?"

She's quiet for a few minutes, and I enjoy the sound of our boots crunching on the snow-covered path.

"It would be filled with much more joy and peace. More time outdoors with brushes and paints capturing the beauty of creation. A lot more time in my imagination, probably more personal satisfaction and enjoyment."

Her voice has a wistful, almost yearning tone. I know without a doubt that it's what she should be doing. I bet she'd thrive in that life. But we all have to make a living, and I'm pretty sure the starving artist tableau has some truth behind it. I can't fault her for choosing work that pays the bills. If she were my girlfriend, though, I'd do whatever it took to make this dream of hers a reality.

Once again, I have to remind myself to drop this line of thought. She's not my girlfriend, and she never will be. I'm only torturing myself by having the idea in my head.

I've never been jealous of Luc before. Not when his career took off, and he bought a fancy car and started wearing custom suits. Not when he went on a date with a minor celebrity. Not even when he officially stepped away from the family business in order to pursue his own career path. Okay, so maybe I was a little envious that he had the courage to face my parents knowing there would be some fallout, but I don't begrudge him his happiness. It's what I wish for everyone I care about. But how he has also found a woman as amazing as Piper who seems to accept him, flaws and all, well... Let's just say the more time I spend with her, the more I see what I'm missing in my life.

It was way too easy to imagine we were on a date when Twigs showed up at lunchtime. And I certainly did nothing to disabuse him of the notion that Piper and I were together. Perhaps I do need to put myself out there again. But maybe I'll wait until I've settled back here. It'd be easier than trying to convince someone I'm seeing to move here from South Carolina. The cold winters and higher altitude might be too much for a Southerner.

We've made our way back to the house, and Piper seems in much better spirits. She heads for the front door, and I follow her. We unzip our jackets and take off our boots in the entryway.

"Look, you two," Elise says, coming down the stairs. "You're standing under the mistletoe. You know what that means."

I freeze, and look up at the green plant tied with a red ribbon. "Uh, I don't think—"

"It's tradition," Nana says, coming in from the living room. "Kiss her, Mac."

My gaze meets Piper's, who has a startled expression. "We don't have to..." I say quietly.

"I don't want to offend your grandmother," she whispers back.

I'm more concerned about how much I really want to kiss her, but if she were my girlfriend, I wouldn't want her kissing anyone else. While I'm still warring between my desires and what I think is the right thing to do in this situation, Piper places a hand on my shoulder, pulling me down toward her while she arches up on her tiptoes. She plants a kiss on my cheek, the scent of warm vanilla cookies invading my nostrils. My mouth waters at the aroma. My eyes close, enjoying the press of her warm lips against my skin.

All too soon, she pulls away and takes a step back. My hand flexes, aching to touch the spot she just kissed, but that might give away how much it affected me, so instead I squeeze my hand into a tight fist and shove it into my pocket.

"Lame," Elise says, turning toward the kitchen.

Nana catches my eye and gives me a wink. What is that about? She pats my arm before heading down the hall to her room.

Feeling disoriented, I grab our boots and beeline for the garage. I remove my jacket, hoping to cool my suddenly hot skin, and pace around in my socks, barely registering the dampness creeping in from stepping on the melting ice Elise must have brought in from skiing.

I'm surprised by the reaction my body had to a simple kiss on the cheek. It felt like my insides were on fire simply from Piper's nearness, and it felt like an electric shock when her lips touched my skin. I can only imagine what I would have felt if we'd kissed on the lips. I fear I might have forgotten myself and wrapped my arms around her, kissing her for all I was worth and forgetting we had an audience. The thought brings up a mixture of longing and guilt. I shouldn't be having these thoughts about Luc's girlfriend. It's disloyal to my brother and feels disrespectful toward Piper. It's not her fault I find her irresistible, or that she checks off all the boxes for my dream woman.

After a stern talking to myself to shape up, I head back inside to find Piper in the living room with Elise, Darcy, and Luc.

"There you are," Luc says, smiling. "I was just telling Piper about that White Elephant when you and Darcy fought over the Game Boy Advance box Uncle John wrapped up that turned out to be rolls of quarters."

I force a smile onto my face even though I feel jealousy's tendrils trying to grab hold of me at the sight of Luc's arm around Piper. Did he see us in the entryway a few minutes ago? He must not have or he'd have said something as soon as I walked in. "I still ended up with fifty bucks, so not a total loss."

"I'm so glad you're joining us tonight, Darcy," Elise says. "It's like I have two big sisters now." She smiles at Piper. "And we finally outnumber the guys, so we can strategize as needed."

"Hey now," Luc says.

"What?" Elise says with narrowed eyes. "Don't think I've forgotten about you and Mac working together to keep me from getting the origami kit. I ended up with a Weird Al box set." She sticks out her tongue.

Luc raises his hands. "Fair enough. I guess that means we'd all better bring our A-game tonight."

After dinner, everyone meets in the living room and sets their gifts on the coffee table. Most things are wrapped in boxes or gift bags. One wrapped gift is as long as the table and a few inches wide. It could hold ski poles or a golf club. Or maybe it's a fake-out. We won't know until someone opens it.

Mom explains the rules for Piper's benefit. The rest of us already know you have to open a gift first and then can steal someone else's and that no gift is safe until the final round, which is when whoever opened the first present gets their pick out of everything. We draw numbers out of the hat. I get number nine—the last one—which is almost as good as going first.

"Alright, who's number one?" Mom asks.

Piper holds up her slip of paper. "That's me."

She grabs a candy cane striped gift bag and pulls out a wrapped box. "Oh, it's a puzzle. Big Rock City. This looks fun."

My eyes widen. "Is that a Magic Puzzle Company puzzle?"

Elise grins. "It absolutely is. There are supposed to be two, but the other one hasn't shown up yet. You better watch out, Piper, or Mac's going to steal it from you. He's a master puzzler."

Piper hugs it to her chest and playfully narrows her eyes at me. "I'd like to see him try."

Everyone laughs.

"I've got number two," says Uncle John, who picks up several boxes and shakes them gently before carrying one back to his seat.

"I didn't know we could feel out the gifts," Piper says.

Luc rolls his eyes. "You're not supposed to, but this is Uncle John's way of making sure he gets a bottle of booze."

Uncle John unwraps the box and, to no one's surprise, it's a bottle of champagne. "I know what I'm having later."

"Not if I get it," Darcy says. "It'll be my New Year's Eve bubbly."

The game goes on with lots of trash talk from the players and plenty of stealing. When Luc opens the gift I purchased, he groans and immediately looks around for something better to steal. I found one of those fancy copies of *Pride & Prejudice* at the thrift store. Unbeknownst to Luc, I used a fifty-dollar bill as a bookmark, but I know he's never going to open the book and find it. He's not much of a reader. He swaps it for Uncle John's bottle of champagne, who exchanges it with Nana's bottle of wine. Nana isn't usually one to steal gifts, and so the round ends there.

Mom opens a fancy cooling blanket, which she trades for the wine and sets off another round of swapping. The following rounds reveal a golf game to be used while on the toilet, an escape room-type game, and a pink photo album with hearts on it. Dad opens the last item, which gets traded around until it ends up with Nana.

I grab the last gift on the table and open it up. Uncle John groans when he sees it's a bottle of bourbon. He currently has the blanket. I look around our circle, trying to decide which gift to trade it for. When the album was opened and revealed photos of strangers, I realized it must be Piper's gift. It was the only other non-new present apart from mine. Not wanting her to feel embarrassed, I trade Nana the liquor for the photo album she ended up with after Elise's round. This results in a few minutes of people—namely Dad and Uncle John—trying to convince her to trade her for their gifts, but she shakes her head and holds onto the bottle. We all know she won't drink it, but are resigned to her ways.

"Alright, Piper," Mom says. "You get to start our final round of trading. You can keep your puzzle or swap it for anything you want. What's it going to be?"

Piper slowly looks around the circle. "As much as I like puzzles, I must admit I love Jane Austen more."

She walks over to Mom and trades her the puzzle for the book. I'm thrilled Piper's ending up with my gift. I can't wait to tell her about the special bookmark.

Mom swaps the puzzle for Elise's bottle of wine. Elise takes the escape room game from Luc, who trades the puzzles for Uncle John's blanket. Uncle John gives the puzzle to Darcy, who has the champagne. Darcy ends the game by declaring the puzzle is hers, which means Dad ends up with the golf game. I catch Uncle John slyly swapping bottles with Nana, who will actually enjoy the champagne. I guess he's not as ruthless as he tries to make everyone believe.

Luc gets off the couch, where he was seated between Piper and Darcy, and comes over to me. "Tough luck ending up with that tacky album."

I shrug. "As long as everyone had fun, that's all that matters."

Luc heads to the kitchen, and Darcy joins him. She says something that makes his head tip back in laughter. She then touches his arm in a way that makes my hackles rise. There always seemed to be an attraction between them, but the family ignored it since neither seemed to want to do anything about it. Though now that Luc's in a relationship, they should probably stop with the casual flirting. I'm about to get up and pull Luc aside when I sense someone next to me.

"Hey," Piper says, pointing to the album at my feet. "I wanted to tell you to check all the pages in there. You might find some welcome surprises."

I pick it up and open the cover. The first page has two pictures of kids making goofy faces. I flip through the plastic pages until I spy a green and gold card. It's a lottery scratch-off ticket. I pull it out of the sleeve.

"There are a few more in there. Hope you win something, but if not, at least it's kind of fun, right?"

I look up at her, reading the uncertainty in her expression. Putting warmth in my smile, I nod. "Nana used to let me scratch off a square or two when I was a kid. There's a thrill in anticipating a payoff. Thanks." I motion to the book in her hands. "You should check the pages. There's a special bookmark inside."

She carefully opens the book and flutters the pages until she finds the bill. She laughs. "You know, most people would think this is the prize," she says, holding it up, "but I collect copies of *Pride & Prejudice* because it's my favorite book, and don't have this one yet. Score for me!"

My chest warms at her admission. I couldn't have known about her collection, but it makes me feel good to know the book will be on her shelf. Maybe when she looks at it, she'll think of me. But why would she want a reminder of her boyfriend's older brother? She wouldn't. I'm letting my thoughts get away from me.

"I'm glad you like it. I thought it was a nice-looking edition."

"I agree. It might be the prettiest one I've acquired so far."

"I'm going to walk Darcy home," Luc calls from the mudroom.

My brow furrows. She lives right next door. I'm sure she can get home just fine. He better not be flirting with her when he's already seeing an amazing woman. Piper yawns and excuses herself to get ready for bed. I clean up the trash from our game and then decide to call it a night, but not before glancing at the door wondering when Luc will be back. How long does it take to walk thirty feet?

I've just come out of the bathroom after brushing my teeth when I see Luc enter his bedroom. He shuts the door behind him, but it doesn't close all the way, so when I'm in my room, I can still hear his voice.

"A few customers are coming to ski tomorrow, and I asked Darcy to join us and make our group an even six so everyone has a buddy."

"Oh," Piper says. "That's fine. What should I do?"

"There are some cool hiking trails if you like that sort of thing. Or you can stay here and read."

Does Luc not know Piper's interests? I honestly didn't think my little brother was that self-absorbed, but he's leaving her alone yet again. And to add insult to injury, he's replacing her with his favorite flirting partner. Why did he even invite her here if he wasn't going to spend any time with her? I'm tempted to march across the hall and knock some sense into him, but I doubt that'd do any good. It'd just make me look like a creepy lurker, which I guess I kind of am. I close my door so I don't accidentally hear anything else that might turn me into a rampaging Hulk looking to smash inconsiderate jerks.

I'm trying really hard to stay out of the situation, but I hate how Luc's treating Piper like she isn't important to him. How can he possibly miss how amazing she is? I'd tell her every day if I were in his position. But I'm not. Even if I'd really like to be.

I guess it's up to me to entertain her while Luc works and flirts with Darcy. Again. We've already been through town, so maybe a long walk on the trails? Hopefully, the beauty of the area will serve as a distraction for her terribly behaved boyfriend. Though there's no way I can assuage my very disturbed conscience without having a serious talk with my derelict brother. He really needs to get his priorities straight before he loses possibly the best thing that's ever happened to him.

Chapter Seventeen

Piper

I hardly slept a wink last night. So many discomfiting thoughts and images ran through my head. I was still a little wound up about falling apart in front of Mac at the art museum after seeing one of Dad's pictures. He didn't seem concerned about my freak-out. In fact, I think it might have been the reason he opened up to me about his struggle with not wanting to work for the family. I honestly think if he talked to his parents, they'd be able to sort everything out.

After all the emotional whiplash from our time in town, I certainly wasn't prepared for what greeted us when we returned home. I'd forgotten the family doesn't use the front door, which is probably why I hadn't noticed the mistletoe attached to the entryway light fixture. Nana looked so excited about people being caught under it, I went with it. Just a little light-hearted holiday fun. Except I had no idea what I'd agreed to.

A little kiss on the cheek shouldn't have been a big deal, but when I leaned in toward Mac, his woodsy scent wrapped around me and went straight to the pleasure center of my brain. I don't know what it is about his cologne, but it makes me want to get as close to him as I can. It's intoxicating.

As my lips touched his skin, I felt a slight friction from his five o'clock shadow, which sent a tingle of delight zipping through my body. Being near such a large, rugged man did funny things to my insides.

And all that was from a simple cheek kiss! I can't fathom what I would have felt if our lips had met, but now there's almost a feeling of regret that I missed out on something huge and wonderful. Which is disconcerting, to say the least. I'd like to believe all these confusing feelings are simply a little holiday magic working overtime, but couple the kiss with the hug we shared earlier, one that made me feel safe and secure in a way I haven't experienced in a long time, and I'm feeling royally discombobulated.

I've been a little cuddly with Lucas on this trip, but my body hasn't responded nearly as emphatically to his touches. If only I could get him to kiss me for real, then perhaps I could find out for sure if we have a chance. Because the way things are going, I'm wondering if perhaps I'm pursuing the wrong brother.

I can't even believe I'm having these thoughts. Maybe it's the nostalgia of the holidays that's got my emotions all stirred up. That, and the fact that the Cahill family has been so amazing to me. This trip has definitely been much better than my original plan of hanging out with Maui all week, even if it is a little perplexing at times.

Today's plan is to walk a trail down by the river with Mac, the guy I'm thinking about in a way that's disconcerting and conflicts with my plan to convince Lucas we belong together. Maybe we shouldn't be hanging out when my emotions are all over the place, but the alternative is holing up in my room, and I just can't abide that when I know how much being outside in a winter wonderland refreshes my soul. Maybe it'll also provide a little mental clarity, something I desperately need.

In my room, I bundle up in my thermals, jeans, and a thick sweater. When I open the door to head downstairs, I hear some tense whispering coming through the crack in the door across the hall. I shouldn't eavesdrop, but I recognize Lucas's voice and can't help myself. I sneak closer, placing my ear close to the opening.

"Inviting Darcy to ski with you today better not be so the two of you can flirt away from prying eyes."

That's definitely Mac's gruff voice.

"Why would you say that?" comes Lucas's affronted reply.

"I doubt I was the only one witnessing your looks and teasing yesterday. It gave me flashbacks to when you were in high school."

What happened in high school?

"It's just a little fun, Mac. Lighten up."

"Do you think Piper would be amused by your antics? She's an amazing woman, and you'd be prudent to keep her in mind at all times."

I feel a little embarrassed overhearing Mac defending me to his brother. It's kind of sweet, but also, did he really see something I should be worried about? Obviously not as Lucas's girlfriend, but as someone who'd like to be. Do I have competition from another person in addition to Lucas's work life? But also, is there competition for *my* heart? It's true I've felt more care and concern from Mac than Lucas recently. That certainly does things to a woman's emotions.

"I know Piper's great," Lucas says. "It's why I'm dating her."

That sounds promising, but maybe he's just sticking to the cover story and doesn't really mean it. If I keep spying on the brothers, my heart might get even more twisted up. As quietly as possible, I tiptoe to the stairs and head down to find my boots. Lucas and Mac come downstairs a couple of minutes later, both giving each other wary looks.

Lucas meets me in the kitchen, wraps me in a hug, and kisses my temple. It feels a little weird, maybe because we haven't established a solid emotional connection. Physical and emotional intimacy go together for me. But we won't be working on any type of intimacy today since we'll be apart for most of it.

"Thanks for being so cool about me working this trip. I know I need to do better at separating work and the rest of my life, and I will once I land this client. You really are great. I promise I'll figure out a way to make it up to you."

"No problem. I want to support you however I can. Slay on the snow today and close the deal you've worked so hard on."

He grins down at me with his million-watt smile, and my stomach gives a reflexive swoop. I spend a second wondering what it'd be like to see that smile every day. Would it wear on me after I've seen it a thousand times or be just as welcome as that first sighting three years ago?

"Good morning, Cahill family!"

Lucas's head swings toward the mudroom where Darcy's just entered looking very cute in her matching ski pants and coat. He releases me and steps toward her.

"Hey, Darcy. I was just about to come find you. We should go so we're not late to meet the clients."

I don't miss the fact that she also receives a million-watt smile and responds with one of her own. Her face is radiant under Lucas's appreciative gaze. I can't help but acknowledge she's beautiful. I feel a deep groove in my forehead and quickly rearrange my expression into something more pleasant. However, Mac's words from earlier make me wonder if he might be right about there being a spark between Lucas and Darcy. I'm not sure how I feel about that.

"Nice sweater," Mac says.

I startle, not having noticed his approach.

"Oh, yeah. It's thicker than the ones I brought. I hope you don't mind."

An expression I can't interpret flits across his face.

"Not at all. You about ready to go?"

"I just need my coat from the garage."

"My boots are out there so we can finish layering up together."

Mac seems so responsible and trustworthy. He gives the impression he's someone who'd thrive in a crisis, making sure everyone made it through unscathed. A "no one left behind" mentality. He's definitely been looking out for me while I'm here, volunteering to keep me company when Lucas has other engagements. I sort of feel like his charity case, but I think that's just Mac's nature—looking out for others and doing whatever he can to help.

Once we're properly protected from the elements, I follow Mac along the road until we reach Yampa River Core Trail near a large frozen pond. We walk past parks and cross over the river several times on the two-hour walk to the end of the trail. When given the choice of retracing our steps or taking a shuttle back to the house, I opt for a return trek. While the cold air has chapped my cheeks, I've enjoyed taking deep breaths of fresh air and seeing all the snow, trees, bodies of water, and mountains. Living in the city, I sometimes forget just how much I love being surrounded by nature.

The first half of our walk was mostly Mac pointing out interesting sights and sharing some of the town's history. Now that we're seeing the same things for a second time, his words have stalled, which means it's my turn to push the conversation forward.

"Did you ever go ice skating on the ponds around here when you were growing up?"

"No. Most of our time was spent on the slopes, though there is an ice rink in the square. I'm surprised you didn't see it when we went skiing."

If my cheeks weren't already pink from the brusque mountain air, they'd certainly be now as I remember my less than graceful trip down the mountain.

"I was probably too traumatized from my disastrous introduction to the sport."

Mac lets out a low rumble of laughter, but suddenly stops when I don't join in.

"I'm sorry. I thought you were joking."

I shrug. "I wasn't. I'm very thankful you were there to help me make it down without breaking something or suffering a concussion. I can't believe how patient you were with me, even in my stupidity."

"You're not stupid." The look he gives me has "stern principal" vibes, and I feel like I should apologize, but he keeps talking. "Luc should have told you what to expect. You're not at fault for his oversight."

I don't think he should blame his brother for my mistake, but he isn't completely wrong that Lucas didn't properly prepare me for this trip. For example, he failed to mention we were coming to a resort his family owned. Definitely something I should have known. He also said nothing about his surly but kind-hearted brother with blue eyes I'm tempted to get lost in. I definitely would have remembered something like that.

"Would you like to go to the square and skate?" Mac asks, interrupting my wayward thoughts.

"Can we?"

"Of course."

I clap my hands together, my spirits lifting. "Yay! I love skating."

"That settles it then."

Mac stops walking and pulls out his phone. After a minute, he nods.

"There's a shuttle stop not too far from here that'll take us to the square."

The ride lasts only a few minutes, and then we're at the skate rental place giving the attendant our shoe sizes.

"If I'd thought about it, I'd have packed my own skates," I say, while we trade our boots for the skates.

"Are you a good skater?"

"I was a competitive figure skater in high school."

I grin at the way Mac's eyebrows hitch up in surprise.

"Whoa. Maybe that's what Luc sees in you."

My brow furrows. "What does that mean?"

"Just that competitive people seem to gravitate toward one another. He skied; you skated."

"And that's the only reason you can come up with for why we're together?"

He must realize he's offended me because he holds up his hands in defense.

"No, that's not what I meant. I think you're great. You're just not his usual type, is all."

"Whose type am I then?"

His mouth gapes open, and he makes a weird strangled sound, but no words come out.

I've finished tying my laces, so I get up from the bench and head out onto the ice. I need to shake the annoyance I'm feeling, or I might say something I regret. It seems like Mac is trying to poke holes in my relationship with Lucas to find a crack that can break us apart. The joke's on him, though, because we're not really together. Still, I'm frustrated he doesn't seem to think we'd make a good couple. Maybe he was making up the whole thing about there being tension between Lucas and Darcy because he's trying to get Lucas to dump me. It doesn't make sense why he'd be against our relationship, and it feels hurtful. I take several laps around the ice, feeling my body settle with each loop, muscle memory taking over.

When I feel more grounded, I look around and see Mac across the ice inching his way around the rink with one hand on the wall. He wobbles slightly, and I can't help grinning. He wasn't kidding when he said he spent most of his time on the slopes. I feel a little bad to be delighting in his struggle, but it's kind of nice knowing I have a skill he lacks for once.

I glide around the ice and slow until I'm almost next to him.

"How's it going?"

He lifts his eyes from the ice in front of him and turns slightly toward me, his hand leaving the wall. This turns out to be a mistake because a second later he's flat on his back on the ice. I have to swallow a chuckle. I plant my skates in the ice and help him back to his feet.

"You really don't skate, do you?"

He shakes his head, then grips my arm with his gloved hand when his feet start to slide out from under him. I steady him as best I can.

"Okay, I'm going to help you out." I remove his hand from my forearm and set it in mine, then hold out my other hand. He places his free hand in mine. "Bend your knees, keep your core engaged and centered over your legs, and look at me while pushing off on your skate."

The furrows in his forehead reveal his apprehension, but he turns out to be very good at following directions. We make a full rotation without falling.

"Are you ready to try it with just one hand and me skating next to you?"

"One more lap with two hands. Please?"

I grin at his politeness. "Sure thing."

We advance to side-by-side skating after the second lap, and eventually he stays upright on his own. After about an hour, he seems to have found his confidence and is picking up speed.

When we take a break for hot cocoa, he asks about my skating career.

"I went to a few competitions and did fairly well. Not Olympic level, but pretty good for an amateur. I even did a few pairs skating competitions, but I didn't like my partner, so that didn't last long."

"Could you do those jumping spins?"

"Axels?"

"I guess?"

"Of course. I could do all the required elements."

He pulls a face. "Sorry, I don't know much about skating."

"It's fine. Want to find out what I can still do?"

His lips quirk up. "Yeah, that'd be cool." He pauses. "I mean, as long as you don't think you'd hurt yourself. I got you safely down the mountain, but I don't think I could rescue you on the ice."

I laugh. "Fair enough. There are too many people to really do anything too crazy, but maybe I could do a spin or something."

He looks around for a second. "If you don't mind relocating, I know where we can go."

The way he says it intrigues me, like what he's suggesting might not be completely legal. Excitement dances through my body.

"What about our skates?"

He shrugs. "I know the owner. He won't mind."

I narrow my eyes. "Are you the owner?"

"I mean, technically, it's my dad..."

I shake my head, but my smile reveals my amusement. "Where are we going?"

Chapter Eighteen

Mac

We're dropped off at Casey's Pond, where Elise and her friends used to play ice hockey, so I know it's safe for skating. There's no one around, which means Piper will be the only one who sees me fall flat on my face, which is sure to happen since there aren't any walls or guardrails out here.

I brush off a fallen log with my gloves so we have somewhere to change back into our ice skates. I venture out onto the ice. I think the last hour really helped me get the hang of it, because I make it all the way around the pond without falling and even get my speed up to a decent clip. Piper glides past me like a natural. She makes a few figure eights, then spins in one spot on one skate. I'm getting a little dizzy just watching her. I make my way toward the center of the pond. Piper skates around me, then goes down to one end before coming back and performing some kind of jump. She looks so graceful I can't help but clap at her feats.

Her smile is so wide her eyes are crinkled into slits. I'm glad I brought her out here. I think she needed some time to let go and have fun. It can't be easy spending a week with a bunch of people you just met. It's definitely not *my* idea of a good time.

I spend a good ten minutes just watching her skate around, doing whatever hop or spin seems to pop into her head. At one point, I realize she's doing a whole routine the way her arms move about rhythmically, and I can practically hear the music.

Piper seems to realize I'm just standing in the middle of the ice watching her because she skates over and extends her hand.

"Skate a lap with me?"

The earnestness in her eyes makes it impossible to refuse. I take her gloved hand in mine, and we skate over to the edge and around the perimeter of the ice. It reminds me of the roller skating parties we had in elementary school and the couples skate under a disco ball. I'm lost in the memory until one of my skates catches on something and I stumble, the front of my skate sticking in the ice while my other leg keeps going. My eyes widen along with my stride. I let go of Piper's hand and reach out for something to stabilize me. Unfortunately, she's the only thing within arm's reach. I wrap her up in a bear hug just as my thigh muscles reach their stretch capacity. I cry out in pain and tip over, landing on my butt and pulling Piper down on top of me. Her elbow rams into my stomach, and the coat layers do little to protect me. I groan, but can't do much else with her body weight still on top of me.

Piper quickly scrambles back up to standing, her forehead creased in concern. "Mac, are you okay?"

I sit up slowly, a hand pressed to my gut. "Just got the wind knocked out of me is all."

Coldness is creeping in through the seat of my jeans. She holds out her hand, and together we get back on our feet. It's then that I realize just how cold my rear feels. The ice must have soaked through the denim. The slight breeze is not helping.

"I'm finished skating," I say, "but you're welcome to keep going. I'll watch from the log."

Her hand on my forearm keeps me in place. I look down into her eyes, which seem to be asking me a question. I have no idea what she might want from me.

"Could you do me one tiny favor before you leave the ice?"

My heart jumps, my eyes flitting down to her lips before I catch myself and bring my gaze back up to meet hers.

"What is it?"

She breaks eye contact, her lips pursing together.

"Forget it. It's stupid."

Her look of defeat only makes me want to know more. "Tell me."

She takes a deep breath like she's steeling herself for rejection.

"Well, it's just...when I was pairs skating, I always hoped I'd get to do the *Dirty Dancing* lift, but my partner wasn't strong enough." Her eyes dart over my torso and arms. "I can't believe I'm even thinking about this. Never mind."

She wants me to pick her up? I know exactly what she's talking about. Elise loves romance movies and has roped me into viewing many of them, this one included. I'm confident in my ability to pick her up, but being on skates worries me a little. Especially if she's flying at me from the other side of the rink.

"After that oh-so-graceful fall, I'm worried I'd slip and one or both of us would get hurt. It doesn't feel safe."

Her mouth opens slightly, her eyes wide. She shakes her head. "You're right. It's a dumb idea. Forget it."

The defeated look in her eyes cracks my resolve. I have an inexplicable urge to make all her dreams come true, but the protective side of me reminds me of all that could go wrong if I give in. Surely there's a compromise to be found.

Against my better judgment, I voice an idea.

"What if I stood in the snow at the edge of the pond and lifted you up from there? You could skate over and I'd grab you before you ran out of ice."

I have to make an effort not to cringe outwardly at my plan. It still sounds sketchy, but it's shredding my heart seeing the despondent look on her face. She looks back up at me with a spark of hope in her eyes.

"That might work. Are you sure?"

Not at all, but I'm finding myself willing to be a little more reckless than usual if it means making her happy.

"Let me change back into my boots first, and then we'll give it a go."

Standing on the edge of the pond, I stomp my feet to pack down the snow and shift my weight back and forth until I feel as sturdy as possible.

"Okay, let's do this."

Piper stands in front of me and shows me where to position my hands. I grab her waist and lift her a few feet off the ground to get a feel for her weight. When I set her back down, she turns and skates out toward the middle of the pond.

"Last chance to back out," she calls.

"No way."

She raises her hand like she's preparing to start a drag race, and I smirk at her adorableness. She drops her arm, and my mouth straightens out. She skates toward me, picking up speed the closer she gets. When she's almost to me, I hold out my arms. Getting a firm grasp of her waist, I bend my knees, keeping my weight evenly distributed over my feet as I lift her up and over my head. She feels light in my arms, and I look up to see if she's got her arms and legs extended, but all that's in my line of vision is her green coat. Her hands aren't on my arms, so I take that as a good sign.

"How are you doing up there?"

"It's just as I imagined."

Her words are tinged with awe, which makes my stomach clench with longing. What would it be like to find ways to bring her joy every day? Unfortunately, it's not my job.

"You can put me down now."

We hadn't discussed how this would work. It'd be a shame to drop her now. I slowly lower my arms, bending my elbows. Her hands find my shoulders for support as I lower her toward the ground. With our arms around each other, this feels very intimate. Our faces are level for a moment, and the grin on her face does something funny to my insides. Realizing my arms have locked and kept her in place, I force myself to continue lowering her until her skates find purchase on the ice. I let go of her waist, clear my throat, then bend down and retie my boot laces to hide the desire for her that's probably written all over my face. Piper steps off the ice and heads over to the log to change back into her boots. When I've gotten a better hold on my emotions, I join her, but when I sit down, it feels like I've made skin contact with ice. I jump up and turn to look at the log, but all I see is some snow. There's a chuckle next to me. Piper has her hand over her mouth, but her eyes dance with mirth. Her gaze wanders down my body to my legs. I reach back to pat my pants and immediately realize something's wrong. I twist around as best I can. Sure enough, there's a huge hole in the seat of my jeans. They must have ripped when I fell earlier. I close my eyes, feeling a little foolish.

"That's an impressive split," Piper says. "Perhaps we should head back to the house so you can change pants."

"Excellent idea." I give her a wry smile, deciding to lean into it. "Talk about being the butt of a joke."

She snorts, obviously surprised by my comment.

"There's the guy I met at the grocery store. Where has he been all week?"

My smile disappears at the reminder. "Chastising himself for flirting with his brother's girlfriend."

Her eyes round in what looks like horror. Was I too honest just then? "You didn't know who I was."

It's true, but I still feel guilty. Especially since I've realized how much I do like Piper. If she weren't dating Luc, I really would ask her on a date. But that's not going to happen because who would be dumb enough to ever let her go? Even Luc has more sense than that.

Piper insists we return the skates before heading back to the house. Even though my rear is freezing, I suggest we take the trail back rather than the shuttle. Spending more time with her is just going to make me fall harder for her, but I can't help myself. I'm a glutton for punishment today.

We're making small talk as we walk through a forest of snowy trees when something cold and wet smashes into my cheek. I look up, thinking snow has fallen from a tree branch above me, but then something hits my shoulder. I turn in time to see a red blur duck behind a tree.

I turn to Piper. "Did you see something?"

Her gaze is focused on something over my shoulder, and she puts her hands up in front of her face just as something white smacks into them. She grabs my arm and pulls me across the path and behind a tree. She's breathing hard, but there's a smile on her face.

"I think we've just been invited to a snowball fight. You game?"

The annoyance I initially felt dissipates. I haven't been in a snowball fight in years. I can't turn down Piper's invitation when I see the excitement dancing in her eyes.

I nod, then bend down and start molding snow into balls. We get a dozen stacked up before I peek around the tree. I just make out two heads across the trail before I duck back behind the tree to avoid getting hit by another snowball. I grab a few from our arsenal and wait for a head to pop out. My first couple of throws miss, but then I peg one kid in the arm.

"Got one!" I shout, grinning over at Piper.

She peeks around the other side of the tree and tosses a ball. It lands far left of the tree the kids are hiding behind. She chuckles.

"Maybe I'll make the balls and you throw them. Your aim is better."

I hit two teenage boys a few times and take a shot to the leg. Suddenly, the other side of the trail goes quiet.

"Did they run away?" Piper asks.

"I don't know," I say, bending down to help with snowball construction in case the ceasefire is only so they can restock. My cheeks stretch with a wide smile. It feels good to play and have fun.

Piper catches my eye and smiles, her cheeks and the tip of her nose pink from the cold. Her eyes sparkle with mirth.

"Oh my gosh, this is so fun! Thanks for doing this with me, Mac."

I can't remember the last time I was this playful with another person. Piper just seems to bring out all the good, fun parts of me. I wouldn't mind having more adventures with her. My brain decides now is the time to remind me that's not going to happen, and my smile drops. Her face gets suddenly serious, and I feel bad for ruining the fun with my sobering thoughts. She drops her head and curls in on herself. What have I done now?

Two snowballs break against her coat, and I turn just as one smacks me in the face. I clock four teenage boys, arms cradling snowballs, and realize we're being ambushed. I move quickly, pushing Piper against the tree and wrapping my body around her. My back and head take the brunt of the assault. There's nothing to do but wait it out. I shiver when snow hits my exposed neck and slides down the back of my shirt.

After what feels like forever, I hear the swish of snow pants receding into the distance. I wait another minute to ensure they aren't returning. My nose itches, and I realize my face is pressed against Piper's hair. She's pinned between the tree and my chest, her arms around my waist and her face buried in my neck. It feels way too good having her snuggled up against me. I allow myself another few seconds of this ecstasy.

"I think they're gone."

"What's that?" Piper's breath tickles my neck and makes me shiver.

"The snowball war is over. We've been soundly defeated."

Though it doesn't feel like I lost. I'd gladly endure another pummeling for more of this.

Piper releases her hold on my waist, allowing me to step back and break our contact.

"Thanks for protecting me with your body. Are you okay?"

She runs her eyes over me like she's searching for injuries, which makes me smile.

"I'm fine, just a little wetter than before."

"And probably colder too. Let's get you home so you can warm up."

Her concern for my wellbeing does something to my heart. I'm used to being the caregiver to everyone else. Someone reversing the roles feels strange but not altogether unwelcome.

She grabs my hand and drags me back to the path. We walk hand in hand for a bit until she realizes we're still touching and lets go. Disappointment fills my chest at the break in contact, even though it makes sense she doesn't want to hold my hand. I'm just the brother of her boyfriend, not some guy she has feelings for, as much as I'd like that to be true. *You're losing it, Mac. Pull yourself together.*

Chapter Nineteen

Piper

When we get back to the house, Lucas and Darcy are already there, curled up next to each other on the loveseat. She laughs at something he says and swats his arm playfully. My body tenses, but surprisingly it's not out of jealousy. Watching them together these last couple of days, I see an easiness between them that Lucas and I don't have. It could be because they've known each other forever, or perhaps it's that undercurrent of attraction you'd have to be blind to miss. Darcy's body is facing Lucas, her shoulders tilted forward like her body's trying to get closer to him. He's leaning toward her as well, his attention completely focused on her. I doubt they even heard us come in.

Mac stops beside me and stiffens. I glance up at him, startled at the fierce scowl on his face. Guess he hasn't missed their attraction. Just like he's probably noticed my attraction to him. When I was skating around the pond earlier, I could feel his gaze on me. It gave me the courage to attempt all my old tricks, and I hit many of them. I may have been a little too courageous when I suggested the lift, but I know he's strong from colliding with him on the slopes, so I wasn't worried about him dropping me. Maybe a little concerned he might lose his footing, but I probably would never get another opportunity to try the move and I was feeling daring. His suggestion of standing in the snow rather than on skates was probably wise. And we nailed the lift! It felt as amazing as I had imagined. Even more so when my arms were wrapped around his neck and I saw a flash of desire in Mac's eyes. And I didn't miss when his eyes flicked down to my mouth. I lost my breath at the intensity of his gaze.

In the thrill of the moment, I was soooo tempted to close that distance, but thankfully—or unfortunately, depending on whether it's my angel or devil speaking—he had his wits about him and reminded me I'm dating his brother. For a split second, I thought about telling him the truth, but I'm pretty sure he'd hate me if he found out I was lying to him. If I let my scheme with Lucas run its course, we can have an anticlimactic breakup, and then maybe it wouldn't be so weird if Mac and I dated. Though he seems so honorable and family-oriented, that I bet he'd never cross that line.

Which really sucks because I've definitely got a crush on him.

Especially after he protected me when we were ambushed during the snowball fight. It was just snow, but the way he didn't even hesitate to wrap his body around mine makes me believe he'd have done the same thing even if the threat was something dangerous.

I was glad to see him let loose and have a little fun with me. I think he spends too much time worried about others and not enough time loving his own life. I seem to draw that out of him, and it makes me feel good that I have a positive effect on him.

I'd thought Lucas, with his slick suits and charming persona, was the perfect person for me. Turns out, I prefer a brooding grump whose actions speak to the amazing man he truly is. Too little, too late, I suppose.

My phone buzzes in my pocket, and I pull it out, smiling when I see it's from Sam. She's been working in watercolor lately, and I'm very impressed by her progress. My favorite medium is oil on canvas, but I've dabbled in watercolor here and there. I open the message. It's not a photo after all, but it makes me chuckle.

> **Sam:** When will you be back? I've missed seeing you. *heart emoji*

> **Piper:** We've only missed one Saturday session, and it's Christmas break. I'll see you in January. Miss you too. *blowing kiss emoji*

> **Sam:** Can't wait!!! *heart eyes emoji* *woman dancing emoji*

"Who's that?"

Mac's gruff voice next to my ear startles me, and I fumble my phone before getting a firm grasp of it again.

"No one," I hiss, worried about drawing attention from the other people in the room.

"I didn't know we gave heart emojis to people who are 'no one.'"

I look over at him. He's got his hands on his hips, and his glare is now turned my way. Annoyed that he's been looking over my shoulder at personal communication, I mimic his stance and narrow my eyes right back before realizing we've got an audience. I motion for him to follow me down the hall to a room that looks like a study. Away from curious eyes, I round on him.

"I didn't know there was no such thing as privacy in this house."

"There isn't when you're *cheating* on my brother."

I rear back, surprised by his accusation. My face twists into an angry frown. I lean forward and poke Mac in his firm chest.

"I'm not cheating on your brother," I say, not bothering to keep my voice low, "and I'm offended you think I'm capable of that. I was unaware you had such a low opinion of me."

I cross my arms, expecting him to back down, but he leans forward until his face is inches from mine.

"Then who's Sam?"

"That's none of your business, but because I don't want your negative opinion of me to taint the rest of the family, I'll tell you. *Samantha* is one of my art students. She's showing a lot of promise with watercolor. Are you happy? Or do I need to show you our text string so you can see all the pictures of the projects she's sent me?"

I unlock my phone and hold it out to Mac, daring him to take it. I can see the conflict in his eyes.

"Just do it," I say, shoving the phone into his hand.

He scrolls through the messages, then holds the phone back out to me.

"I've also got a student named Joey. Do you want to read through those messages as well, just to be sure? Or what about my co-worker, Charles? Maybe we're having a secret office romance."

He shakes his head, then meets my fiery gaze. "I'm sorry, Piper."

He seems to be genuinely remorseful, but I'm hurt he even thought I would do something like that.

"Whatever," I say, snatching the phone back. "At least now I know what you really think of me."

He flinches at my rebuke. "I don't think that about you. You've done nothing deserving of my suspicion. You are obviously an honest and genuine person. I apologize for questioning your integrity. I let my own insecurities color my judgment."

It's my turn to flinch, but I manage to keep a neutral expression. While I'm not a cheater, I'm certainly not being honest with his family right now, and it's really bothering me. These people are so wonderful. I hate the idea that my subterfuge may hurt someone in the end. Maybe I should try to convince Lucas to tell his family the truth. Then he'd be free to pursue Darcy if that's what he wants.

"What's going on in here?"

Lucas is standing in the doorway, a concerned look on his face. He catches my gaze. "Everything okay?"

"Fine," I say, purposefully not looking in Mac's direction. "Can we go up to the room for a sec?"

"Sure," he says. He takes my hand and leads me up the stairs. I close the door behind us before telling him about my confrontation with Mac.

"It's fine if you're talking to someone," Lucas says, "just maybe don't do it where snooping eyes can see."

"What? No! I'd never. Sam really is a woman."

He shrugs, not concerned in the slightest.

"But, um..." I say, wondering how to approach the subject delicately. "If you're interested in Darcy, we can break up right now so you can pursue her."

He shakes his head a little too emphatically. "We're just friends. It's just been a long time since we've seen each other, and it's been nice to catch up."

"Mmm. I may not be a body language expert, but you looked like you two were leaning toward one another down on the couch."

He chuckles. "The small couch probably just made it look that way."

"Are you sure? Because even if you may not be interested, I think Darcy is. If you don't share her feelings, maybe cut back on the flirting, yeah? Your brother's definitely noticed the chemistry between you two."

That sobers Lucas up. "Oh. Mac thinks something's going on? Thanks for telling me. I'll be more careful."

It's on the tip of my tongue to push him to end the charade, but then I remember I'm only here to be his supportive girlfriend. If he wants to keep pretending, then that's what I'll do. It's only a couple more days. I can handle that.

When we return to the main floor, dinner is on the counter and people are making plates. Lucas laces our fingers together and pulls me into the kitchen. He hands me a plate, gets me a drink, and sits next to me at dinner. He's so attentive and kind, I almost wonder if he's been body snatched. I guess the fear of our secret being exposed was enough to straighten him up.

After dinner, Susie announces it's Christmas movie night. Elise's name is drawn from a bowl to choose the movie, and we all move to the living room to watch *While You Were Sleeping*. Lucas pulls me over to the loveseat, inviting me to lean against him while he casually drapes his arm over the couch behind me.

It's been a long time since I've seen this movie. I get goosebumps at the similarity of Lucy's story to mine. We're both orphans celebrating Christmas with someone else's family. Toward the end, my stomach twists when I realize I can empathize with her just wanting to belong to others and feel loved and accepted. People do crazy things when they're lonely. Including agreeing to fake date a co-worker.

Luckily for Lucy, she figured out her feelings before it was too late. And because it's a rom-com, she ended up with the man she truly loves. Somehow, I don't think my life is that charmed. Real life is never like the movies. At least I'm only pretending to date Lucas. I can't imagine how we'd untangle our web of untruths if his family thought we were engaged.

Christy: Are you and Lucas official yet? *prayer hands emoji*

Piper: No. I think he's interested in someone else, actually.

Christy: Oh no! *sad face emoji* I'm sorry.

Piper: It's actually okay. After spending a few days with him, it's possible Lucas is not the one for me. *shrugging emoji*

Christy: *raised eyebrow emoji*

Christy: Does this have anything to do with his hunky brother?

Piper: No…but also yes?

Christy: ???

Piper: It's complicated. Enjoying time with your family?

Christy: Definitely not as exciting as staying with the Shire family. Did I tell you Brooks's brother blew up the microwave right before we left?

Piper: No! There's no end to the excitement with them. *exploding head emoji*

Christy: Makes me kind of glad the most exciting thing to happen here thus far has been a rousing game of charades.

Piper: I bet. See you in a few days!

Chapter Twenty

Mac

Yesterday was kind of a disaster. I offended Piper multiple times, even calling her a cheater, which turned out not to be even remotely true. Definitely not my best moment. I don't even know why I accused her. If it was my subconscious trying to put some distance between us after the intimacy of the snowball fight, it certainly succeeded. And she really doesn't seem like someone who would do that. Luc, on the other hand, was looking way too cozy with Darcy when we got back. He must have realized how things looked because he was much more attentive to Piper last night. Though maybe she had a chat with him about his behavior when they were in their room. I wouldn't put it past her. She certainly put me in my place last night. And rightly so. I feel pretty terrible about my behavior, but don't know how to make things right.

I haven't seen Piper this morning, so she must be sleeping in. Maybe I should avoid her to keep my foot out of my mouth. I'll relegate myself to the basement just to be safe. At the bottom of the stairs, I hear low talking coming from the lounge where I was headed. I recognize Nana's voice and creep closer. Luc sits in a chair across from Nana, perched on the arm of the sofa.

"You've found a good one, Lucas Henry."

Ooh, she's using his middle name. This must be serious.

"Thanks, Nana. She's certainly not like anyone else I've dated."

Boy, is that right. Piper is not only the most attractive woman on the planet, she's also smart and talented. I looked up her dad's work online, and it is incredible. I also searched Piper's name and was amazed to learn she'd gone to Rhode Island School of Design in Providence and then the Royal College of Art in London, graduating with honors. That search led me to a portfolio of stunning landscapes and portrait paintings. She really should be painting as a career. How in the world does she not believe she could make a living with her art?

"You'd be smart to hold on to her," Nana says. "And in that vein, I've decided it's time to give you my engagement ring."

My breath catches in my throat. Nana wants Luc to propose to Piper? I mean, I get it. He'd be stupid not to marry her, but my stomach plummets at the thought. It would be pure torture seeing her at every family event knowing Luc gets the pleasure of her company every day. He doesn't deserve her. He was just lucky to have met her first.

A thought niggles in my brain. What if Piper says no? Just because Luc has a ring doesn't mean it's a done deal. He's used to getting what he wants, so I wonder how he'd handle that rejection. Of course, perhaps she'd say yes. He leads a charmed life after all. Why wouldn't an amazing woman say yes to marrying him?

Abandoning my plan of hiding out in the basement, I head back upstairs and run straight into Piper. I stifle the groan that climbs up my throat when I see she's wearing my robe over her pajamas again. What have I done to deserve this punishment? Someone kill me now.

"Hey, Mac," Piper says flatly, regarding me with wary eyes.

I guess she's still mad about last night. I can't blame her. Might as well apologize again while we're standing here. It can't make things any more awkward than they already are, and maybe it'll help me feel a little better about everything.

"Hi, Piper. I'm really sorry about last night. I don't know what came over me. I honestly don't think you'd do that. You are a trustworthy person."

Something flickers across her face, but then she takes a sip of coffee. I notice she's got the Christmas Vacation mug again. When she takes it away from her face, I notice her eyes are a little red. Has she been crying?

"Don't worry about it," she says. "You were just standing up for your brother. I think it's nice you have his back like that. And I promise you I wouldn't do anything to deliberately hurt Lucas."

I appreciate her generous interpretation of the events. If I'm honest, part of the reason I confronted her was because I secretly hoped she wasn't that interested in my brother. If not, maybe she'd consider dating me. But that's a ridiculous and horrible thing to think. Piper is a good person. Her confirmation that she won't hurt him only makes my stomach sink further. If Luc asks, she's definitely going to say yes. Just put me in the grave now, because my hope is dead.

I really should leave her alone, but I just can't help myself. She's much more subdued than usual, and Piper not being her normal bubbly self bothers me more than it should. I can't come right out and ask her if she's been crying, but surely there's an appropriate way to phrase my concern.

"Is everything okay? You aren't as chipper as usual."

She starts to nod, but then stops. "It's the anniversary of my father's death. I'd hoped that being here this year would be enough of a distraction, but it's not."

Her eyes well up with tears, and I desperately want to wrap her in a hug, but don't know if that would be welcome right now. My fingers twitch at my side, and I grit my teeth to keep myself from reaching out to her.

"There you are, sleepyhead," Luc says, brushing past me as he reaches out to give Piper a hug. He presses a kiss to her temple, and I turn away, my jaw clenching with jealousy. "I've got a surprise for you. I thought we could go on a date to the hot springs today. What do you say?"

"I say yes!" Piper says.

Her voice has the proper enthusiasm, but I can still detect a hint of sadness in her tone. Luc doesn't seem to notice, though. At least he's returned his focus to the proper woman, even if he seems oblivious to her emotions at the moment. It sounds like she needs a distraction, and Luc is definitely the person to give her one. I shouldn't be mad about that.

Besides, Luc could definitely benefit from a strong woman like Piper, who will challenge him and make him a better person. I bet she'd do that for anyone she was with—I mean, who can deny her radiant personality? She's like a walking ball of joy. Every time I'm around her, I have to actively keep my facial expression neutral or I'd be smiling like a fool and everyone would know how I really feel about her.

After breakfast, Luc and Piper head out to the hot springs. I'm already dreading their return. My brain helpfully conjures the image of Luc on one knee in the water and Piper's wide grin as he slides the ring onto her finger. I try to occupy myself with the puzzle, but all I can think about is how much more fun it is when Piper's sitting next to me. I wonder if she's been able to put the terrible anniversary to the side and enjoy the attention Luc is sure to be giving her. My stomach churns at the thought of them cuddled up and kissing in the hot springs.

I give up on the puzzle and head outside for a brisk walk. Maybe the cold air will knock some sense into me. Piper isn't mine. Never has been. Never will be. I have to acknowledge that fact and move on. Maybe I should join a dating site or see if one of my buddies will set me up. Neither of those options sounds appealing.

When I return to the house, my fingers and toes are numb, but nothing has changed about the dread in my chest. The house is silent. It must be quiet rest time, as my parents like to say. I grab a book from the living room and sit down in the recliner. After an hour, I realize I haven't read a single word. My mind has been thinking about a certain brunette and wondering if she's sporting a new ring yet. An eternity later, I hear voices in the mudroom.

Lucas and Piper come in, looking happy and relaxed. The distraction must have worked. I can't see Piper's hands, so I refrain from offering congratulations until I know for sure the deed's been done.

"I need to do something upstairs for a bit," Luc says. "Where will you be?"

"I think I may grab a book and blanket and read out on the deck."

He grabs her hand and squeezes affectionately. Her fingers are ring-free. He hasn't asked her yet.

"Great. I'll come join you when I'm finished."

"Sounds good."

She gives him a sincere smile that makes my heart twist with jealousy. *Knock it off, Mac. You're better than this.*

I turn back to my book, but my mind cannot concentrate on anything but wondering when Luc might pop the question. Just the thought makes my heart pinch. What if he's not ready? They've only been together six months. That's not a very long time. It's a tiny shred of hope for my soul. He seems to like her, but maybe he doesn't love her yet. Though how anyone could resist Piper's sweet spirit and not fall for her is unfathomable to me. I've been staring at the same page for ten minutes when Luc passes through the living room and heads out to the deck.

Unable to remain still, I hop up and grab a cookie from the kitchen as an excuse to spy on whatever might be happening out back. Yes, I'm a glutton for punishment. Piper and Luc are wrapped in a tight hug. Does this mean what I think it means? Mom comes into the kitchen and snags a cookie from the container.

"What are we watching? Is there a cardinal out back?"

I turn. "What? No. Nothing. Just lost in thought."

She peers out the window and then squeals. I turn back. Luc has the ring in his hand, extended out to Piper. My heart drops out of my chest.

Chapter Twenty-One

Piper

I'd been able to push all reminders of today's date to the side while we swam in the hot springs and Lucas talked about his experiences growing up here in Steamboat Springs. It sounded like a pretty idyllic childhood. He even admitted Darcy had been his first kiss when they were in middle school. It was fairly innocent, and they never dated, but from the fondness in his voice, I can tell he thinks highly of her.

I actually enjoyed getting to know Lucas outside of work and our charade. While he can make me laugh, it solidified my recent ruminations that we wouldn't make a good couple after all. He's very driven in his career, and I don't want to compete with it for his attention. Even if he were to pull back after landing this client, I just feel like we're moving in different directions. His big dream is staying in Denver and having a thriving career. He's not interested in raising kids or exploring the wider world.

I've realized I'd like to do some traveling again. I've been in one city for five years—my longest stint ever—and would like to get back out there and be inspired by the beauty of the world. Being a mom is high on my dreams list as well. I've also discovered Lucas likes competitions a lot more than I do. He said that being on the slopes again makes him want to race again. While we were at the hot springs, he challenged me to see who could do the most underwater flips (him), hold a handstand the longest (me), and name the most state capitals (him). Dating him would probably be fun but also exhausting. Plus, it turns out he doesn't really like sweets apart from his coffee creamer. Not even chocolate.

I know Mac doesn't share his brother's aversion to sugar with as many cookies as he's taken down this week. I bet he ate three-quarters of them all by himself. And in his current career, he's done plenty of traveling and doesn't seem eager to come home and stay in one spot.

The way I keep comparing Lucas to Mac is even more confirmation we're not the right fit. So, our fake breakup after New Year's will be perfect because neither of us will be heartbroken.

Despite the entertainment and distraction of Lucas and the hot springs, as soon as we're back at the house and I'm settled into a chair on the back deck with a book and blanket, my mind floods with thoughts of that terrible time. The voicemail from the hospital. The rush to get back to the States. Crying on the plane and freaking out the surrounding passengers. The sympathetic look on the nurse's face when she told me he was gone. Laying numbly on the couch in his house for days, wishing the nightmare would end.

If it weren't for his neighbors bringing me food and sitting with me while I ate, I don't know what would have happened. I didn't even go back to London to get my stuff. My roommate packed everything up and shipped it to my dad's house. I couldn't live in a place with so many memories of happier times, so I sold it, moved into an apartment, and got a cat for company. And then took the first job I was offered.

I guess I've sort of been in survival mode these past five years. Being here with Lucas's family has shown just how little progress I've made in moving forward since Dad's death. Yes, I've got my friendship with Christy and the painting class on Saturdays, but I'm teaching rather than doing. Dad wouldn't be excited about how I'm currently living. He'd want me to pursue painting like I'd always dreamed. Knowing he'd be disappointed makes me sadder. Perhaps this trip was the wake-up call I needed. However, the idea of striking out on my own and sinking or swimming based on my artistic skills feels scary. Everything feels so much more daunting when you don't have a support system.

I swipe at the tears coursing down my cheeks. The sliding glass door opens behind me, and I quickly wipe the blanket over my face.

"Whoa, must be an emotional book," Lucas says when he sees me.

I rub under my eyes and stand up, dropping the book on the chair with the blanket. The cold seeps through my clothes, and I wrap my arms around myself.

"What's the news?" I ask, changing the subject.

He grins. "I did it!"

My eyes widen. "The clients signed the deal?"

He nods, and I squeal, leaping forward to give him a hug.

"Congratulations, Lucas. That's so awesome!"

He laughs. "Thanks. It feels good to have all that hard work pay off."

I let go and step back. "I'm sure."

He puts his hands in his pocket, his brow furrowing. He pulls out one hand and holds up a gorgeous pear-shaped diamond solitaire. It looks an awful lot like an engagement ring.

"Lucas. What's that?"

He chuckles, probably at my wide-eyed, slightly terrified look. "It's not what you think. Well, it kind of is. It's my grandmother's engagement ring."

Instinctively, I lean away from his outstretched hand. If you'd told me a week ago I'd be less than excited about seeing a ring in Lucas's hand, I'd have said you were crazy, but even though we had fun at the hot springs, it confirmed we'll never be more than friends. There weren't any zips or zings seeing Lucas in a swimsuit or having all of his undivided attention for once. In fact, the hug we just shared felt very platonic. And I'm okay with that. "Why do *you* have it?"

"Nana thinks you're great. She told me you were amazing and that I'd be a fool to let you get away. Hence, the ring."

"And what did you say?"

He shrugs. "I agreed you were a lovely person and promised I'd do it when I felt ready. Which, of course, will be never, but only you and I know that at the moment."

I exhale a relieved sigh, glad we're on the same page. Now that I know I'm not in danger of being proposed to, I lean closer for a better inspection of the ring but freeze when I hear a shout from inside the house. We both turn toward the kitchen window. Susie's face is practically pressed up against the glass, a wide smile on her face.

"Uh oh," Lucas says, drawing my attention back to him. "How do you feel about getting pretend engaged to me?"

My stomach drops. "What?"

"You know what this must look like to her, right?"

Mouth agape, I search for a way out of this situation. "But you're not even on one knee. Maybe..." I trail off, unable to come up with an alternate explanation.

He sighs. "Nana probably told everyone she gave me the ring. I know I just said this was never happening and I really hate to ask you to do this, but if we don't let this play out, the rest of this trip is going to be really awkward and I'm going to have to deal with pitying glances from everyone. The whole point of your being here was for me to avoid that. Please pretend this is real, and we'll break up after New Year's like we agreed."

My thoughts immediately go to Mac. If I say yes, this will mean nothing can ever happen between us. There's no way he'd go after his brother's former fiancée. But if I say no, I'd either have to leave immediately or be on the receiving end of death glares for the next two days. It feels like a lose-lose situation for me, but at least I can help Lucas win by agreeing to this insane plan.

"Fine." I hold out my hand, palm up.

"Thanks. I owe you." Instead of placing the ring in my hand, he reaches out, cradles my hand, and lowers to one knee. "Piper...I don't know your middle name...Miller, will you pretend to get engaged to me?"

I chuckle despite the tightness in my chest. "It's June, and yes, I will be fake engaged to you."

He slides the ring onto my finger. It's a little big, but that doesn't matter since this is only temporary. □

Lucas stands up.

"I'm going to kiss you now because we have an audience."

My heart speeds up. This is what I'd hoped would happen not even a week ago. And yet now I'm dreading what's about to happen. He leans in and presses his lips to mine, lingering for a few seconds before pulling away again. Not even a tiny tingle in my body. My cheek kiss with Mac had more sparks than that. Confirmation that my crush on Lucas is over. My stomach twists uncomfortably with the realization that this fake proposal is equivalent to the final nail in the coffin of any possibility of something ever happening with Mac. However, existential dread is not what one is supposed to be feeling after being proposed to, so I lock my feelings away and paste on a smile when I hear the sliding glass door open and Susie's voice.

"Oh my goodness! Congratulations, you two." She hugs Lucas first, then wraps me in a tight hug. "Welcome to the family, Piper."

Her words are a stone in my gut. Nana hugs me next before taking my hand and admiring the ring.

"I knew this would look perfect on you. Did you know my Harry proposed to me with this ring on a carousel at the State Fair?"

"That sounds so romantic."

She looks wistful. "Oh, it was. We had fifty-one wonderful years together. I hope you and my grandson will be just as happy."

Ugh, I feel terrible. At least I won't have to see their faces when Lucas tells them it's off. I can't imagine having to witness their disappointment.

John, Elise, and Hank are next to offer their congratulations, with Mac bringing up the rear. His face has taken on a tortured expression, so even though he says he's happy for us, it looks more like someone just told him his dog died. There appears to be a hint of sadness in his eyes, but maybe I'm just projecting my own feelings. If Mac were standing next to me, and he had placed this ring on my finger, I doubt I'd have this queasiness in my stomach. But it's too late for that kind of thinking. I have to live with my choices.

It doesn't get any easier when Darcy shows up for dinner and her face drops for a second when she hears the news. I was definitely right in thinking she likes Lucas. Well, maybe this will turn out to her benefit. Thinking she's lost him, when she finds out we've broken up, maybe she'll have the courage to tell him how she feels. I can definitely understand whatever disappointment she's currently feeling because I'm right there with her. She puts on a brave face and congratulates us.

I use the opportunity to ask her a few questions about herself and learn she's a nurse at a hospital in Denver. Lucas suggests we all go out for drinks after New Year's. Darcy agrees, but I can tell she isn't thrilled about the idea of being a third wheel.

"I want to throw a party for you two tomorrow to celebrate the engagement," Susie says.

"That's unnecessary, Mom," Lucas says.

"It's not every day we have something this exciting happen in the family. Love should always be celebrated."

Oof. The guilt over our charade is piling up. It wasn't so bad when we were just dating, but a fake engagement takes things to an entirely different level. It doesn't seem right to deceive such lovely people, but I promised Lucas I'd help him out, and he's who I should be loyal to.

"That's so kind of you, Mrs. Cahill, but Lucas is right. We're just happy to share the news with those he's closest to. Besides, it's Christmastime. We don't want to pull people away from their family gatherings just for us."

She purses her lips. "I suppose we can wait until January for an official engagement party, but we'll still have a family celebration tomorrow evening."

I suppose that's the best we can do without coming clean. Lucas must agree because he accepts his mom's pronouncement.

"Great," she says. "That's settled, and now we can get on with tonight's family activity. We're going to draw partners from the hat and paint each other's portraits."

"What?" Elise says. "I thought we were making gingerbread houses."

"Change of plans. The holiday twist to this activity is that you have to make the portraits Christmas themed. You can add a snowman to the background or put a Santa hat on your person. Something fun like that. Mac gave me the idea earlier today, and I thought it would be fun to try something new."

I glance over at Mac just as he looks away from me. Did he set this up because of our conversation? It's been a long time since I painted a portrait, but this feels pretty low-stakes and silly. It might even be fun.

Names are drawn from a bowl, and Nana is my partner. We sit down across the table from one another. It's kind of hard to see her with the canvas propped up on the table in front of me, so I have to keep peeking around the side. Darcy is on my left, and Lucas is across from her. Mac is on my right with his dad as his partner. Elise and Susie are partners, and John has made himself the honorary judge since there's an odd number of people. The winning team will be chosen based on their success with the Christmas theme, so no one feels bad about their skills. Susie sits down at her canvas and yells, "Go." I pick up my paintbrush and get started.

Chapter Twenty-Two

Mac

I'm struggling to concentrate on the painting I'm supposed to be working on. Every time I blink, my brain flashes to the image of watching Luc sink to one knee. My chest squeezes uncomfortably at the memory. It feels like my worst nightmare has come true.

I know that sounds dramatic for a stoic guy like me, but I've never connected with someone the way I have with Piper. She seems like the one person who can help me loosen up and be myself instead of the usual stone-faced responsible eldest son who anticipates everyone else's needs persona I've adopted over the years. It was almost like I had permission to care for myself for once without worrying about other people.

Now I'll always be worrying about whether my brother is treating his wife as she deserves. And there's nothing I can do about it either. I can't ask him if he's paying attention to her wants and needs, putting her ahead of his work responsibilities. Well, I could, but it would be weird and unwelcome.

Perhaps I should quit the Air Force and work at the ski resort just so Piper can have at least one reliable support in her life. I shake my head at the thought. She's got my parents and extended family on her side now. She'll probably be just fine.

So maybe I should *stay* in the Air Force and have a reasonable excuse for missing family events where I'd have to see Luc and Piper together. Unfortunately, I won't be able to avoid their wedding. If Luc asks me to be his best man and I have to stand up front and watch Piper walk down the aisle toward me but not actually to me, I may lose it.

A sharp crack interrupts my thoughts. The paintbrush I'm holding has snapped in two. Whoops. I get up and toss it in the trash, grabbing another pack of brushes off the island before re-taking my seat.

Mom, who's sitting to my right, leans over to look at my picture. "Interesting choice, Mac."

I harrumph, but dip my brush into the brown paint and start working on adding antlers to the top of Dad's head. I turned him into Rudolph the Red-Nosed Reindeer. The blue eyes and dark hair with a smattering of gray only slightly resemble my father, but I never claimed to be an artist.

When the antlers are finished, I sneak a peek to my left. I freeze, stunned by Piper's painting. It looks just like Nana, down to the sparkle in her eyes. The background is the kitchen behind us with its garland, lights, and Christmas kitsch. There's even a tray of sugar cookies already decorated like some of the ones we made earlier in the week. How has she created something so amazing in so little time?

"Whoaaaa..." slips out before I can stop myself.

She pauses her work on Nana's sweater, which has elves putting presents on Santa's sleigh, just like the one Nana wore for caroling.

"What?"

"You—that's amazing, Piper." What I wanted to say was, "You're amazing," but caught myself in time.

"Thanks."

She goes back to her work, and I force myself to stop staring. I add a couple of ornaments hanging from the antlers to distract myself from Piper's amazing painting. Mine certainly won't win any awards, but it should make the family smile.

When the timer goes off, Mom orders all paintbrushes down like this is an actual competition. Each pair is instructed to reveal the canvases to their partner on Mom's count. Elise frowns at her wonky face turned into an ornament on the tree. Though she didn't do much better turning Mom into a snowman. Dad likes my reindeer, and his painting of me flying down a hill on a sled makes me smile. Luc's and Darcy's paintings look like abstract expressionism, but there's lots of red and green paint, so they're technically on theme.

Nana gasps when she sees Piper's picture, her eyes filling with tears.

"This is beautiful, Piper. You truly have a gift."

She sure does. It's a shame she's working in an office making slides for the sales force rather than spending hours working on creative masterpieces like this. She needs to paint full time. I know it isn't my place to say something to her, but Luc doesn't seem to appreciate Piper as much as he should, and I doubt he even noticed the way she lit up while she painted. There's a niggle in my brain that says I would cherish and champion her better. It's probably just jealousy, which means I ought to keep my mouth shut.

"May I keep it?" Nana asks.

"I think that's the point, right?" Piper says.

"I'm sorry about yours, dear. I really tried my best."

She holds it out to Piper, who grins and then shows the rest of us. Nana turned Piper into a ballerina balancing on one foot, holding a nutcracker in front of a giant Christmas tree.

"It's so lovely, Nana. My dad took me to see *The Nutcracker* one year, and I told him I wanted to become a ballerina. Now I am one. Thank you!"

Piper gives Nana a hug, and my heart squeezes at the genuine expression of joy on her face. She really is the best. I turn away to hide the scowl stealing over my face. Why does Luc get to be with my perfect woman? He really sucks sometimes.

I clean up all the paint supplies so that I don't have to watch Piper and Luc be lovey-dovey with one another. By the time I'm done, having refused several offers of help, the downstairs is empty. Everyone must have gone to bed. I try to do the same, but toss and turn more than sleep.

I lay in bed the next morning listening to the sounds of people moving around. The smell of coffee finally lures me downstairs. Thankfully, Luc and Piper don't seem to be up yet. I know I'm supposed to be happy for them, but with how terribly I slept, I'm feeling more dour than usual. I'm afraid I may say something inappropriate or regretful.

I decide to walk into town and look for an engagement present. It'll keep me out of the house for a few hours, and the cold air outside ought to wake me up. Maybe I can act my way into feeling celebratory about their exciting news. I highly doubt it, but stranger things have happened.

Everything I see in town makes me think of Piper. One of the antique stores has a leather-bound copy of *Pride & Prejudice* with hand-drawn illustrations inside. There's no way I can leave it there knowing she'd be thrilled to own it. I buy it, deciding to find something equally personal for Luc. Which would be...maybe a nice leather briefcase for work? Or a new ski jacket? No, neither of those says, "Congrats, you're getting married!" to me.

As I'm walking past a store, my eyes catch on an object in the window. The memory it elicits is too strong to ignore. Without hesitation, I go in and buy it. That now makes two gifts for Piper and zero for Luc.

I sigh, realizing my mission is futile. Buying gifts for the couple will not change how I'm feeling right now. It's going to take time for me to even consider being happy for Luc. Why does he need a gift anyway? He already has everything he needs. Which, not coincidentally, is everything I want.

Chapter Twenty-Three

Piper

My stomach has been in knots all morning thinking about the engagement dinner this evening. I was mostly okay with deceiving everyone about me and Lucas dating because couples break up all the time. But now that it's escalated to an engagement, and the family wants to celebrate, I feel extremely guilty. These are lovely people who don't deserve to have their hearts jerked around like this. And knowing how fond Nana is of me already…it physically hurts thinking about her disappointment at the coming turn of events.

Obviously, I can't just go through with everything and marry Lucas simply because I love his family. While there's a tiny bit of me that wouldn't think that'd be so bad, that's a level of deception I just can't abide. Besides, I don't want to marry someone I'm not in love with.

My eyes dart over to the empty chair at the table where Mac should be sitting. He's been gone all morning and is currently missing lunch. No one else seems to care, laughing and joking while we eat. I'm the only quiet one at the table. Well, that's not completely true. Darcy is also noticeably low-energy. Right now she's staring into space, her face downcast. She was pretty somber last night during painting as well. I doubt I'm the only one who can tell she's not thrilled about our engagement. And she doesn't seem to be alone. Mac seemed grumpier than usual last night. I'm not exactly over the moon about the recent turn of events either, but what can I do?

When everyone is finished, I help clean up and then excuse myself to my room to call Christy. I really need someone besides Lucas to talk through everything with. Thankfully, she answers on the third ring.

"This better be good. I was just about to win at cards."

"Lucas proposed to me."

"He *what*?!"

I pull the phone away from my ear, cringing at the volume of her voice.

"Calm down. It's not real. His mom saw us together and thought he was proposing, so we went with it."

"Wait. I thought the whole point of this charade was to show Lucas how awesome you are."

I shake my head even though she can't see me.

"No. I mean, yes, initially, but like I texted you a few days ago, I've realized we're just meant to be friends. Besides, there's some-one here who definitely has heart eyes for Lucas, and I'm thinking about trying to get them together."

"How are you going to do that? It'd be awfully suspicious if you tried to set your fiancé up with another woman."

I sigh. "You're right. But, Christy, you should have seen how happy his family was. Well, except for his brother, but that's another story. His grandmother had tears in her eyes. It's her ring I'm wearing right now."

"You've got a ring?"

My phone beeps with a FaceTime request. I accept, and Christy's face fills the screen.

"Let me see!"

I grin and hold my hand up in front of my face.

"That is gorgeous! Too bad you're gonna have to give it back."

"Returning the ring will be a piece of cake compared to saying goodbye to his family. They're all so amazing, and it's been so long since I've felt this welcomed and accepted."

She gives me an empathetic smile.

"I'm sure. But you've still got me."

"And I'm very thankful for you."

"Now what's this about Lucas's brother not being happy for you?"

I shrug. "I don't know. I mean, he's a bit of a grump around his family, so they probably haven't noticed anything, but I've spent enough time with him this week to know something's definitely off with him. I wonder if he's figured out this thing with Lucas is fake and he's mad we're scamming his family."

My stomach twists with fear. If he knows we're lying, will he say something? I know we'll never see each other again after this week, but I hate the thought of him thinking I'm a terrible person. Even if I were to come clean now, it would only lower his opinion of me. I'm out of luck either way I play it, so I might as well stick to the plan for Lucas's sake.

"Oh, girl. I'm sorry. Good thing vacation's almost over. You're still coming with me and Brooks to the company's New Year's Eve party, right?"

I roll my eyes, though it might be nice to have something to do other than sit at home and eat Oreos with Maui. "I guess."

We talk for a few more minutes and then I lie on the bed, wondering how I got to a place where I'm lying to a bunch of kindhearted people. I honestly wouldn't mind being part of this family. I've unwittingly burned that bridge by agreeing to Lucas's scheme, but how was I to know how easily they'd welcome me into their family and how refreshing it'd be to feel like I belonged somewhere again? If nothing else, it's shown me how lonely I've been and the importance of having a community. Growing my inner circle will be the top priority when I return home.

After allowing myself a few more minutes of wallowing, I drag myself off the bed and head back downstairs. Hank, Susie, John, Elise, and Nana are watching a movie. Lucas and Darcy are sitting at the puzzle table, but have their heads together whispering instead of fitting pieces together. There's still no sign of Mac, though why do I care? If he's not here, I don't have to worry about him blowing my cover if he's figured it out. What I need is some time in nature to clear my head.

"I'm going to take a walk," I say.

Darcy pops up from the table. "Mind if I join you?"

I don't have a reason not to accept, so we gear up in the mudroom. When we get outside, Darcy points down the hill, and I nod, trusting her to know where she's going. We walk for a few minutes, and I allow the muted sound of our boots on the snow-covered pathway and a few bird calls to calm my thoughts.

"I don't think I've said 'congrats' to you yet," Darcy says, breaking the silence between us.

"Oh, thanks."

"You know, part of me thought Lucas and I would end up together eventually."

The skin on my neck prickles, and my stomach squeezes. "Oh, yeah?"

She chuckles, sounding nervous. "I know it's stupid. He was my first kiss when we were teenagers. Whenever we were together, I felt like we were a team. Like we were meant to be, you know?"

My mind flicks over to the memory of skating on the pond with Mac. "Things felt easy between you."

She smiles. "Yeah, you get it." She pauses, her smile dropping. "I guess that's what you feel with him too."

Guilt sucker punches me, and I have to work to keep my face neutral. Does Lucas have any idea Darcy's been carrying a torch for him? I've suspected it all week, but this is irrefutable confirmation. Knowing this ruse is hurting yet another person unnecessarily almost feels like too much. I'm tempted to blurt out the truth, but my promise to Lucas keeps my lips sealed.

Only two more days and then I'll be back in Denver, dancing in a ballroom with co-workers and strangers, and can leap into a new year and leave the craziness of this last week behind.

I have no idea how to respond to Darcy. Thankfully, I spot Mac heading up the path in our direction and use that as a diversion.

"Hey, there's Mac."

Darcy waves. "Mac!"

He nods in acknowledgment.

"Where have you been?" Darcy asks when we meet, looking pointedly at the bag tucked under his arm.

"Town."

"A man of many words," Darcy says, with a teasing lilt to her voice. "I need to dart into town right quick. Would you walk with Piper back to the house?"

He meets my eyes briefly, then looks back at Darcy. "Sure."

"You okay with that?" she asks me.

"Yeah, I'm fine. Go do your thing."

I'm actually not fine with it. Mac's proximity has caused goosebumps to rise on my arms, and my heart is banging against my rib cage. I'm not sure if it's excited to be near him or nervous that he's going to confront me about the lying. Either way, I hope I don't have a heart attack.

Darcy continues down the path, and I turn around to head back up to the house with Mac. We walk in charged silence. I'm sweating under my coat, just waiting for him to say something. If he asks, I don't know that I'm going to be able to keep my mouth from spilling the truth. I hate all this subterfuge. I'd make a terrible spy.

"Can we sit for a bit?" Mac says, nodding toward a bench up the path.

I nod, afraid my voice will give away how nervous I feel. My whole body is tense, ready to admit everything. We sit and I cross my ankles to keep my legs from bobbing up and down.

"Here," he says, handing me the bag he's been carrying. "I didn't get you anything for Christmas, so this is a Christmas-slash-engagement gift."

"You didn't have to, but thanks."

"Don't thank me until you open it. You might hate it."

I give him a skeptical look. I've known him for less than a week and have learned how observant he is. Whatever is inside this bag will probably be something I didn't know I needed. "I doubt that."

I pull out a heavy, rectangular object wrapped in layers of tissue paper. When the wrapping falls away, I gasp at the blue leather book bearing the title of my favorite novel. I slide it out of its sleeve, a huge, gold peacock filling the cover. I carefully flip through it, awed by the drawings inside.

My eyes don't want to look away from this incredible gift, but it deserves proper recognition. I turn my face up to Mac.

"This is beautiful. Thank you."

The words seem inadequate, especially because I've done my research on special editions of *Pride & Prejudice* and know how much this book probably cost him.

"Where did you find this?"

He hikes a thumb down the path. "In town, actually."

I shake my head, amazed. "Wow."

He nods toward the bag. "There's something else in there."

I can't imagine anything else as amazing as this. I carefully return the book to its sleeve and place it back in the bag for safekeeping before removing the second object. It's lumpy and oddly shaped, also wrapped in tissue paper. When I get it unwrapped, I'm stunned by the object in my hand. It's a snow globe with two people ice skating on a pond surrounded by trees. It looks just like me and Mac, except the female figure is wearing a pink skating leotard and the man's in black. I'm immediately transported back to the pond. My eyes prick with tears, and my heart twists with regret.

In another life, I would never have agreed to Lucas's scheme, Mac and I would have met in some serendipitous way, and we'd live happily ever after. Too bad I'm stuck with this one.

"Thank you, Mac. These are amazing."

That's an understatement. These are the most thoughtful gifts I've ever received.

"You're welcome."

I return the gifts to the bag, then rub my frozen nose. Mac must notice because he stands up and offers his hand, pulling me to my feet. "Let's get back to the house and warm up."

"Hey," Mac says as we near the house, "I wanted to say that your portrait of Nana was incredible. How did you make something that detailed so quickly?"

I shrug. "I'm actually pretty rusty, but I must admit it felt good to paint again."

"Why don't you? Paint as a career, I mean."

I cut him a look. "You know. Because of my dad."

"No offense, but do you think your dad would be happy that you're in a job you don't love that doesn't even touch a tenth of the artistic talent you have?"

Oof. Talk about getting smacked in the face with the truth. "No, he wouldn't."

"Don't you think you owe it to him and yourself to make a go of it?"

My hackles rise. There may be some truth in what he says, but who is he to give me advice?

"Says the man who's afraid to tell his parents he'd rather fly than run the resort. When are you going to live your own truth?"

He scowls, stopping inside the garage and squaring up against me. "That's not the same. I have people I'm responsible for. I can't just abandon my family."

I take a step forward, ready for a fight. For somewhere to funnel the anxiety and hopelessness I'm feeling. "I think your family would be just fine with you pursuing your own happiness. You don't have to sacrifice yourself for them. They wouldn't want that for you."

"How do you know what my family wants? You've known them less than a week."

"Maybe so, but I know how loving and generous and supportive they are. They'd want you to be happy. They wouldn't abandon you for choosing your own dreams. And it's pretty special to have that in your life. I hope you'll never have to know what it's like to be alone."

"You're with Lucas now. You aren't alone anymore."

I scoff, wanting to tell him how wrong he is. "Yeah, whatever."

Needing to be alone, I scamper up to my room and shut the door. I take out the book, running my hand over the beautiful cover. Grabbing the snow globe, I shake it and watch the white flakes fall around the smiling couple. Tears well up in my eyes.

There's a knock at the door and then Lucas peeks his head in. The smile on his face drops when he sees me. He shuts the door and comes over to the bed, dropping to his knees and reaching for my hands.

"What's wrong?"

I sniffle. "I don't know if I can lie to your family anymore. They're all so wonderful, and I feel terrible."

His forehead furrows. "Can you just get through tonight? To-morrow we head back, and then I'll tell everyone some story after the new year."

I suck in a breath, trying to get myself under control. "Wh-what could you possibly tell them that won't make either of us look like a bad guy?"

If I'm never going to see them again, what does it matter if I'm seen as a villain? Because Lucas doesn't want pity. But if he does the breaking up, he might be on the receiving end of ire instead. I think he hasn't completely thought this through.

"I don't know, but I'll figure it out."

He leaves, but I stay in the room, my mind spiraling over my time here this week. I'd just expected to have some holiday fun and perhaps come out of it with a new boyfriend. How was I to know I might run into the man of my dreams and that, unfortunately, he wouldn't turn out to be my fake boyfriend?

Mac sees me in a way no one else ever has. He's shown me in little ways that he's supportive and appreciates my interests and passions. He seems to remember everything I say and looks for opportunities to make me smile. We've had fun together, and I adore his family and their traditions. He's a caring person, and I feel terrible deceiving him. Especially because I know he feels guilty for flirting with me earlier in the week.

I could see us building a beautiful life together if we were given the chance. He could continue to fly, and I could go with him to wherever he's stationed and paint to my heart's content. I wouldn't be alone because I'd have someone who truly knows me and loves me.

But that will never happen because I've been lying to him. Even if I tell the truth, he'll hate me forever, and I can't blame him. But at least he wouldn't have to feel guilty anymore. And it'd give Darcy space to be honest with Lucas. Right now she thinks she's lost him for good, and that really hurts my heart because I know exactly how she feels.

There's too much at stake to continue this farce. Lucas's family deserves the truth, and I've come to care about them in a way that gives me courage to be on the receiving end of their anger and hurt. Lucas may be displeased with me, but it's the right thing to do.

Chapter Twenty-Four

Mac

I feel terrible about confronting Piper the way I did. She's right; I have no idea what it's like living without a support system. My whole life I've had people who love me and encourage me and let me pursue wild hairs. Not just any parents would let their teenager get a pilot's license. And if mine hadn't, who knows where I'd be right now? Probably running the resort like they want me to. But they've allowed me to become my own person and do things on my own timeline. I really should be honest with Dad about where my heart is leaning; I just don't want to disappoint him after everything he's done for me.

But that conversation will have to wait because it's time to head out for Luc and Piper's engagement dinner at Cafe Diva. I head upstairs to change into a nice shirt and slacks. When I come out of my door, I meet Piper in the hallway. She's wearing a black-and-white striped dress that hugs her curves and makes my mouth go dry. She startles when she sees me. Have I made her nervous around me? Is she afraid I'll attack her again with how I think she should live her life? Obviously, it's not my place. I don't know what it's been like for her all these years without family.

"Piper, I'm so sorry about earlier. I didn't mean to attack you, and I don't want my future sister-in-law to fear me. What can I do to make it up to you?"

She blinks a few times, her cheeks paling. "There was truth in your words. I appreciate your caring enough to be honest with me."

I swallow thickly, feeling guilt grow inside at her words. I haven't lied to her, but I've definitely been doing my darnedest to hide my feelings from her. Not sure how honest that makes me.

"And actually," she says, "there's something I'd like to be honest about with you."

My curiosity is piqued. What's she going to say?

"The limo's here," Mom calls. "Let's go."

I groan, realizing this conversation has to be put on pause. "Let's talk later."

Piper presses her lips together in a frown but nods.

When we get to the restaurant, we're guided to a private room. Mom picks everyone's seat, placing Luc and Piper in the middle of the table. I'm across from him and next to Darcy.

"Raise your glasses, please," Mom says, holding up a glass of champagne. "A toast to Piper and Luc. May you have a long and happy life together."

It pains me to drink to that, but I do. It doesn't slip my notice that Darcy puts her glass down without drinking. Maybe I was half right in thinking there was something going on between her and Luc. It's possibly just one-sided, like my infatuation with Piper.

Of course, I've realized what I feel for her is more than simple infatuation. I truly care about her. I hate that she's not pursuing her dream and, if I could, I would do whatever was required for her to be a full-time artist. I'd find a place to live with a room that gets lots of natural light or set up track lighting or do whatever it takes to give her an art studio. I'd buy her all the supplies and canvases and paints and brushes she wanted. But that's not in my future, nor will it ever be. I desperately hope Luc supports and encourages her painting like I would if she were mine.

"I know you're headed home tomorrow, Piper," Elise says, "but I talked to the owner of Something Blue and we can go in early and try on dresses."

The thought of Piper in a white gown has my heart in my throat. I bet she'll make a beautiful bride. Elise's suggestion makes everything feel way too real. A glance next to me at Darcy's blanched face gives me little comfort. When I look back at Piper, her mouth is right next to Luc's ear, saying something that makes him frown.

"No, please," Luc whispers loudly, staring at Piper with pleading eyes.

"I'm sorry," Piper says quietly. She clears her throat. "Can I have everyone's attention?"

Luc covers his face with his hands. What's going on?

Piper stands, her hands clasped together so tightly her knuckles are white. "First, I wanted to say that I have loved spending this time with all of you. It's been a long time since I've been surrounded by people at Christmas, and it felt so special." She clears her throat and wipes under her eyes. Is she crying? "This week I've felt like I belong here, like I'm someone's sister, niece, daughter, and granddaughter, and it touched something deep in me." Her voice cracks at the end of the sentence, causing a lump to form in my throat. "You've all been so kind to me, and I feel terrible for what I'm about to say."

Dread wells up inside. Her gaze pings around the table, landing on mine.

"Lucas and I are not getting married. We aren't even really dating."

What? My brain tries to understand her words, but nothing is adding up.

"But Luc told us a month ago he was bringing his girlfriend," Mom says.

Piper nods. "He *was* dating someone, but they broke up, and he asked me to fill in. I didn't think it'd be a big deal, but then I came and met you all. I told myself it was fine because people date and break up all the time, but now that you think we're engaged, it feels like too much. I don't like deceiving others. Especially not after I got to know you and fell in love with you."

Her eyes meet mine for a second, and then she looks away again. My heart hammers in my chest. Is she talking about my family in general or someone more specifically?

"Luc, is this true?" Nana asks.

He nods glumly.

"Why didn't you just tell us the truth?"

"I didn't want to look like a loser. What kind of man gets dumped by his girlfriend right before Christmas?"

"Oh, sweetie," Mom says. "I'm so sorry."

"And there it is," he says, glaring at Piper. "The pity."

What's his problem? He somehow conned Piper into enduring a vacation with strangers, and he's mad when she's so tenderhearted and compassionate that she feels bad about being deceptive?

"I guess that's my cue," Piper says, pushing in her chair. "I really am sorry. I will cherish this time with you all forever."

"You're leaving?" Nana says.

She nods and heads toward the door, pausing at Nana's seat to lean down and give her a kiss on the cheek. Nana whispers something in her ear. Someone grabs my arm. Darcy's staring at me with wide eyes, her fingers squeezing my bicep like a boa constrictor. "Did Luc and Piper just break up?"

"Can you really break up if you're not actually together?"

She shrugs, smiles, then grabs her champagne glass and takes a long drink. My gaze stays fixed on the door Piper just walked through, trying to sort through everything I just heard.

Chapter Twenty-Five

Mac

After a very awkward dinner, where Luc refuses to talk about what was going through his head when he cooked up this scheme, we return to the house and everyone scatters. Darcy pulls Luc out onto the deck. Elise goes down to the basement. Mom and Dad huddle together on the loveseat in the living room while Uncle John pulls up a recording of the evening news. Nana heads off to bed, not seeming very troubled at all. She gives me a hug and a wink before she goes. I'm not exactly sure what that's about, but Nana has always marched to her own drum.

I consider sitting at the puzzle table but know I won't be able to concentrate so I head up to my room, my brain already sifting through the past week and bringing up things that seemed off at the time but are now giant, waving red flags I can't believe I missed. It should have been obvious how little Luc knew about Piper. From the fact that she couldn't ski to the lack of sensitivity about her family history. The man didn't even think to get her a Christmas present, for Pete's sake. Yes, he said he'd ordered something, but I've known Luc his whole life, so I know when he's lying. And yet, I ignored all those inner twinges that something wasn't right. Probably because my jealousy that Luc was with Piper colored all of my impressions.

I think back on our time together when it was just the two of us because Luc was busy with work. It makes sense now why Piper wasn't bothered that he wasn't spending time with her. She was just playing a part. Which means our interactions were probably genuine. The playfulness in the grocery store, the heated moment on the pond after the lift, the snowball fight cuddling, the kiss under the mistletoe. I certainly felt a spark between us. Did she? I couldn't ask because she was dating my brother. Except she wasn't. So what does that mean now?

It means she lied to me, which I certainly don't condone, but I know how charming and persuasive Luc can be when he wants something. Can I really blame her for agreeing to his harebrained scheme? She didn't know I would fall for her. There's no planning for something like that. But I have no idea how she feels. Sure, we had some fun, and we shared a few deep conversations. I liked that she stood up to me when I confronted her about her career choices and called me out for not going after what I want either. She certainly wasn't wrong. I do need to talk to my dad about the future. I also think Piper and I would be good together, good for each other. I can certainly forgive her for the ruse, but can the rest of my family?

These are the thoughts swimming around in my head long into the night. I finally fall asleep knowing what needs to be done.

The next morning, I find Dad in the kitchen reading the paper while he drinks his coffee. I grab a mug, my heart twinging when I realize I'm holding the *Christmas Vacation* one. Sitting down at the table with my coffee, I take a deep breath to fortify myself for the conversation I've put off for far too long.

"Hey, Dad. There's something I want to talk to you about."

He puts down the paper and meets my gaze. "What's up, Mac?"

Oh boy. This is even more difficult than I had imagined. I force myself to maintain eye contact.

"You know how it's coming up on time for me to re-up with the Air Force?"

He nods, taking a sip of coffee.

"I know before I joined, I said I'd come back and run the resort so you can retire, but that was before I realized just how much I'd love flying and training new pilots. I'm not quite ready to give that up."

He sets down his cup. "Are you saying you want more time?"

"Yes." I grimace, knowing that's not the whole truth. "No. I'm saying I don't want to run the business."

He looks down at the table, silent.

"I'm really sorry, Dad."

He meets my gaze again. "How long have you known this?"

"Quite a while." I feel terrible about having kept his hopes alive.

He sighs. "Well, that's a relief."

Wait. What? "You're not mad?"

The corners of his mouth tip up.

"Of course not. I want my kids to be happy. The fact of the matter is, Elise has been hounding me to take over. She worked at the front desk for years in the summers and interned with me throughout college. She knows the business inside and out, but I'd promised the GM job to you. Since you don't want it, she can step right in. I can finally retire, and your mother and I can go on a nice vacation. Maybe somewhere tropical. I hear Fiji is quite nice in January."

My mouth hangs open in shock. Now that he's said it, of course it makes sense for Elise to take over. She loves the resort and knows everything about it from top to bottom. Sometimes I forget that, although she's my youngest sibling, she's all grown up. My shoulders relax. I'm not letting my family down after all. It feels like a giant boulder has been lifted off of me. I had no idea how much responsibility for our legacy had been weighing me down when all along there was a perfect solution.

"That's awesome. Elise will be fantastic. And Fiji sounds amazing."

He claps me on the shoulder. "So, how long do you think you'll stay in the Air Force?"

I shrug. "I don't know, maybe until I don't love it anymore."

"So, forever then," he says, and we both laugh.

Luc comes into the kitchen and drops an envelope on the table in front of me.

"I found this in my room."

I don't recognize the handwriting on the front, but it's distinctly feminine, which makes my heart speed up. There's no way I'm reading it with an audience, so I grab it and head out onto the deck, keeping my back to the door so no one can see my face while I read.

Dear Mac,

I'm so sorry for lying to you, for lying to all of you. When Lucas proposed the fake dating idea, I thought it might be nice to have a distraction from my loneliness and the dreaded anniversary. I had no idea how wonderful and inviting your family would be. They made me feel loved and like I belonged somewhere, and I haven't felt that in a really long time. And then I didn't want to give up that feeling, so I continued to pretend. Even when I realized I had feelings for you, I tried to compartmentalize things, even deluding myself into thinking perhaps after all this was over, you'd be able to forgive our little ruse and give me a chance. But I realize how selfish and unreasonable that was. Even though I'll never see you again, I couldn't leave without at least telling you I've fallen in love with you. I think you're wonderful. I love how fiercely you care for and protect your family. You are so good at noticing and providing just what someone needs. You made me feel seen and valued, and I'll never forget that. I wish you all the happiness and joy life has to offer, and whenever I see a plane in the sky, I'll think of you.

Love, Piper

It feels like I've just been slammed by a Mack truck. Piper has fallen in love with me? It's hard to believe, even though it's written on paper. It was too much for me to hope she felt anything between us, but now that I know she does, I want to track her down and tell her I feel the same way. Except I have no way of reaching her. But I bet Luc does.

Rushing back into the house, I pace through the downstairs, but there's no sign of him. I check his room, but it's empty. My heart lurches when I see my robe in the closet, the Christmas sweater Piper borrowed hung up next to it. She's gone, but that doesn't mean it's forever.

I sprint back down the stairs and stop in front of Dad, who's still in the chair reading the paper.

"Where's Luc?"

"He went skiing with Darcy."

I try calling his phone, but it goes to voicemail. However, the *Find My People* tracker Mom forced us all to use shows me exactly where he is on the slopes. I race back upstairs and throw on my ski clothes. When I return to the first floor, Nana is sitting in the living room.

"Mac, come here a minute, please."

I huff out a breath, not wanting to waste any time, but I can't refuse my grandmother. I force a smile onto my lips. "Yes, Nana?"

She pats the seat next to her on the couch, and I plop down even though my muscles are twitching for action.

"You seem out of sorts. Does it have something to do with Piper?"

My eyes widen in surprise. "How did you know that?"

She chuckles. "Women's intuition. That and I saw how you two looked at each other."

"What do you mean?"

"If you weren't casting longing looks her way, she was trying not to stare in your direction. You were both glowing after your outing together the other day. I don't think it was just the fresh air that put a sparkle in her eyes. She said it was gliding across the ice, but I bet it was something more."

If she noticed something between us, I wonder who else saw it. It's hard to doubt anything she's saying after reading Piper's note. There's no harm in telling the truth now.

"I was definitely smitten with her, but I promise nothing happened. I thought she was dating Luc, and I'd never interfere in someone else's relationship."

She pats my hand. "I know that, honey. It's why I gave Luc the ring. I smelled something fishy, but couldn't put my finger on it. I figured it might freak him out enough to tell us what was really going on. But I was wrong."

My heart drops. "Does that mean you didn't really like Piper?"

She smiles. "I didn't like her for Luc. I thought she'd make a better match for my other grandson. What do you think?"

I swallow thickly and nod. She grabs my hand, gives it a squeeze, and winks. Has she been manipulating things all this time? But how?

"What I want to know," she says, "is how you feel about her."

I don't hesitate. "I'm in love with her."

She beams up at me and then reaches into the pocket of her sweater. She turns my hand over and drops something into it. I look up at her, wondering if she's suggesting what I think she's suggesting.

"What are you going to do about it?"

"I was just about to chase Luc down on the slopes to get her phone number."

"Then why are you sitting here chatting with me? Go!"

I laugh, then jump up and head out of the house. It takes me an hour to chase down Luc on the slopes, and when I do, I find him and Darcy kissing on a bench at Thunderhead Lodge. While I'd like to have a conversation with him about that, now is not the time.

"I need Piper's phone number."

His brow furrows. "What's up? Everything okay?"

"I hope it will be. I just need to find her."

"You're in love with her, aren't you?" Darcy says.

How does she know? Whatever, it doesn't matter.

"Yes. I need to tell her I'm not mad about anything that happened and just want to be with her."

My phone dings with Piper's number. When I try to save it in my phone, I realize I already have it from our day on the slopes when a woman took our photo. How could I have forgotten? Impulsively, I pull up the photo, a lump forming in my throat at her smiling face. I make the call, my heart banging against my chest like a caged animal trying to escape. It rings and rings before going to voicemail. Nothing I want to say is fit for a message, so I hang up.

"She didn't answer. Do you know where she lives?"

Luc shakes his head, but then pauses. "I know where you might find her tomorrow, though."

The thought of having to wait one more day hurts, but it's better than never seeing her again. "Tell me."

When I get back to the house, I head up to my room to pack. A soft knock on the door interrupts me. Elise comes into the room and takes a seat on the edge of my bed.

"What's this about you staying in the Air Force?"

I press my lips together, realizing that my decision to step away from the family business means it'll all eventually fall on her shoulders.

"I'm sorry, Els. I just can't do it."

She frowns for a second, then laughs.

"Do you think I'm mad? I'm definitely not. I'm excited for the opportunity to show Dad and John what I'm capable of. I've been preparing for this for years. While you were out flying planes, I was learning the business from the ground up, working in various sectors of the resort to fully understand all the mechanics. Yes, it's going to be a lot of work, but I love Steamboat Springs. You were made to be a pilot. I was born to manage people. You probably just haven't noticed because when you look at me all you see is your baby sister. But I'm all grown up and up to the task."

I'm surprised by her speech, but she's right. I really haven't paid much attention to how she's changed over the years. I was too busy with my own life and job concerns. I nod, appreciating her honesty.

"You're right. I know you'll be a great general manager."

"Thanks, big bro. Now, I hope the state of your room means you're leaving us to go get Piper."

My mouth drops in shock.

"What?" she says, clearly amused. "You think I couldn't tell you had the hots for Luc's girlfriend? You don't have as good a poker face as you think."

I frown. "Do you think everyone else noticed?"

She chuckles. "Nana definitely did, but I think the rest of them were too thrilled with the idea of Luc possibly having something to get his mind off of work for once."

I sigh, embarrassed at having been more transparent than I thought.

"Don't worry about the family, though," she continues. "Focus on what's most pressing—telling Piper how you feel."

I shake my head, amazed at how perceptive she is.

"When did you get so smart?"

She grins. "I've always been smart, but thanks for finally noticing."

Chapter Twenty-Six

Piper

I've been heartsick for two days. I still feel awful about lying to Lucas's family. The wounded look on their faces will haunt me for a long time. Maybe I shouldn't have left without saying goodbye, but I was so embarrassed. I couldn't bear to hear their new opinions of me after finding out I was a liar. And I know I sort of left Lucas in the lion's den, but his family is decent and will forgive him for his role.

I left notes of apology. And returned the ring, of course. Though I couldn't bear to give back the gifted copy of *Pride & Prejudice* or the snow globe. I hope Mac doesn't mind. They're a beautiful but painful reminder of what I want but can never have.

When I left the restaurant the other night, I was worried some-one might chase after me. Or worse, that the entire family would return to the house while I was still there and glare at me while I slunk out the front door. Thankfully, they must have continued on with their dinner, though I feel bad for how awkward that must have been for Lucas.

I don't know why he was so worried about their reaction to his getting dumped. Now that I know the Cahills, I'm confident they would have been sensitive to his feelings and not big jerks like he insinuated. Maybe Lucas was just avoiding dealing with his own feelings about the breakup. I certainly know a thing or two about trying to outrun pain. I also know it never works.

I packed my stuff in record time and scribbled a couple of notes while I waited for the car to arrive and take me to the airport. Thankfully, there was a commercial flight to Denver with seats still available that night. It made me glad I'd only packed two suitcases for the trip.

If nothing else, this past week has helped me to see that I've been living on autopilot for a while. I haven't dared to go after what I want. Now that I've had a glimpse of how rich my life could be, I'm no longer content with what I've been settling for. Which means it's going to be a new me in the New Year. Only one more hour to go!

Christy steps up beside me at the bar where I'm waiting for a sparkling cider.

"I just won a hundred bucks at roulette!"

"Congrats. How's Brooks holding up?" Her husband isn't a fan of large parties, but he enjoys the casino at the company's shindigs. All the parties Elite Creative throws have a casino, open bar, large buffet, raffles, and a dance hall with a deejay. There's something for just about everyone to enjoy.

"He's been at the blackjack table for over an hour, making friends with the dealer."

I smile. "Think you'll be able to get him onto the dance floor before midnight?"

She rolls her eyes. "I doubt it."

The bartender hands me my drink. "Then why don't we go have some fun? The deejay's been playing some bangers."

"Yessss!"

When we get to the dance floor, couples are swaying to a slow song. The two of us hug the edge, hoping the next one is more our speed. When I hear the first beats of "Party in the USA," I set my glass down on a tray and grab Christy's hand, pulling her to the middle of the floor. We throw our hands up and sing along, thrilled when the music transitions into "I Gotta Feeling" by the Black Eyed Peas.

While we're screaming the lyrics and dancing, my gaze snags on a familiar face. I'd forgotten Lucas might be here. It takes me a second to recognize the woman on his arm. Seeing Darcy makes me smile. The coziness of their posture gives me hope she finally told him how she feels. I don't want to make small talk with them—things might be a little awkward this soon after the engagement dinner—so I turn my body away from them, close my eyes, and try to lose myself in the music.

After two more upbeat songs, the deejay announces she's slowing it down by request. Elvis's voice croons about fools rushing in. I look over at Christy, but she's staring at something over my shoulder. I turn to see what's so interesting and almost smack into a broad, suited chest. My eyes travel up to intense blue eyes, and my breath catches.

Mac holds out his hand. "Would you dance with me?"

I'm so stunned I don't think I can move, but somehow my hand finds his and he pulls me close. Our feet move together, my mind reeling at the fact that somehow he's here. How did he know where to find me? And *why* is he here? My heart, currently trying to beat out of my chest, seems to know the answer, but my brain is more skeptical.

His arms tighten around me, and I melt into the embrace, resting my head on his shoulder. He smells of the woods in winter with its crisp, clean air. I'm determined to enjoy this little slice of heaven I've been given in case this is just some vivid dream I'm hallucinating.

In the middle of the song, I feel the whisper of a breeze across my forehead. I lift my head from Mac's shoulder and realize he's quietly singing the words to the song. My heart squeezes when his lips whisper, "I can't help falling in love with you." My eyes dart up to his and find him gazing intently at me. They flick down to my mouth, and my breath catches. The air around us feels charged. Something in my soul whispers, "Something life-altering is about to happen. Get ready."

My pulse pounds in my ears. My tongue darts out to wet my lips, and something ignites in Mac's eyes. In the blink of an eye, his mouth presses firmly against mine. My eyes close and I press up onto my toes, kissing him like I was lost in the desert and his lips are my first taste of water in forever. I relax into his embrace like I'm home while my body lights up on the inside, energized by his touch. My arms tighten around his neck, pulling him even closer to me, our lips never breaking contact.

I don't know how long we stay locked in the heated embrace, but eventually the catchy beat of "You Make My Dreams (Come

True)" by Hall and Oates breaks into the haze of Mac's kisses. I smile against his lips before pulling back to look at him.

"Uh, Mac? The song's over."

He blinks, his arms loosening. "It is? Oh, sorry."

He lets go and takes a step back, his hands sliding into his pants pockets. Now that the initial shock of seeing Mac has worn off, I can truly appreciate how dapper he looks in his black suit and tie. I don't know if I like him better like this or in Christmas sweaters. Honestly, I'd find him hot in a clown costume. My fingers itch to reach out and wrap myself up in him again, but perhaps we should talk a bit before there's more kissing. My brain is still struggling to believe he's right here in front of me.

I'm finally able to tear my eyes away from admiring his physique only to realize he's been staring at me like a hungry wolf. My cheeks heat at his intense stare.

"You look beautiful," Mac says.

"Thanks. You too."

The corners of his lips tip up. "Can we go somewhere to talk?"

My stomach flops. This is what I was just thinking, but what does he want to discuss? Is he going to yell at me for lying to him? Whatever he wants to say, it can't be too bad because he just kissed me like I was the oxygen he needs to live. And we might as well get everything out in the open once and for all. I reach for his hand, enjoying the feel of it in mine, as I lead him out of the dance hall and over to a small alcove away from the games tables and bar. I lean against the wall and pretend to be casual, even though I'm freaking out inside.

He reaches a hand toward mine, but pauses and puts it back down by his side. Disappointment washes over me, but I hold still, sensing he needs to be in charge of whatever is happening right now.

After another few seconds, his hand darts out and grabs mine. I watch his hand move from cradling mine, to twining our fingers together, back to holding it gently in his own. He raises our hands in the air between us, then bends down to place a gentle kiss on the back of my hand. His mouth lingers there, and I close my eyes and relish the contact and the warmth of his breath against my hand when the kiss ends. He lowers our hands but doesn't let go. I force my eyes open and back to his face. My heart skips a beat.

The look of anguish and longing on his face causes dread to well up inside. This is goodbye, isn't it? Well, at least I'll have the memory of his kiss to keep me warm for a while. I try to steel myself when he opens his mouth to speak, but find I'm woefully unprepared for what comes out.

"Piper, I'm in love with you."

I freeze. That doesn't sound like goodbye. I blink several times, trying to process the words.

"I'm sorry. What?"

"I knew the moment I met you that you were going to be someone special in my life. Of course, for a while there it about killed me to think you might end up as my sister-in-law. I'm so glad you won't be because I want you all to myself."

His words are finally beginning to sink in, and it occurs to me he's making a speech I probably really want to hear, so I focus in on his mouth. Those full, tantalizing lips that make me weak-kneed. Nope, too distracting. My gaze roams up to his eyes, which are still staring intensely at me, searching my face for something. Maybe proof that what he's saying is getting through. What was he saying again? Oh, yes. He wants me all to himself. My body tingles at the thought.

"You are so smart and talented, beautiful, funny, and sweet. You charmed my family in a week. It took me only a few seconds to see how amazing you are. Piper, I want you. I need you. I love you. Be mine forever?"

Oh my gosh, that almost sounded like a proposal. Which would be crazy, right? He's most likely suggesting that we start dating, something I'm definitely all in for. But would I say yes to marrying a man I've only known a week? Granted, it's been an event-filled week with lots of togetherness, and I've seen how well he cares for his family. It's natural to think he'd care for me just as well. And it's true that I have fallen in love with him. So maybe it wouldn't be so far-fetched after all. But he's not asking me that. At least, not yet. And we should probably go slow and let things flow naturally.

"Yes. Yes! Of course, I'll be your girlfriend."

He frowns, then seems to come to a realization.

"Wait, I think I did that wrong."

And I'm confused again.

"What are you talking about? Don't you want to date me?"

"No. I mean, yes." He shakes his head. "Just give me a sec."

He lets go of my hand and turns away, muttering to himself. He turns back around after a few seconds, takes my hand and drops to one knee, pulling a ring out of his pocket. A ring I recognize. Someone gasps, and I look past Mac to see we've got a small audience. Lucas has his phone out, Darcy's staring at us with her hands clasped together giving us heart eyes, and Christy and Brooks are next to them. Christy's mouth is open, her eyes wide with surprise.

I refocus my attention on Mac. He clears his throat.

"I know this might seem really soon. And we can have a long engagement if you want, but Nana once told me you just know when you've found the person you're supposed to be with. My whole heart tells me I've found her. I have loved learning more about you this week and admire your artistic ability and your ice skating skills. You are the Christmas competition queen and puzzle master. I want to know everything about you and champion you in all things. I want to love you and prove my love for you for the rest of my life. Piper June Miller, will you marry me?"

Before he's finished, tears are streaming down my face, and I'm nodding like a bobblehead doll.

"Yes, Mac."

I don't even give him a chance to get up. I jump at him, kissing him for all I'm worth. He's sturdy enough I don't knock him over. He wraps his arms around me, then stands up while we're kissing, leaving my legs dangling a few inches off the floor. But I don't mind. I've had a dream or two about kissing Mac for real, and the reality is so much better than my fantasies.

Eventually the sound of clapping and cheering registers, and I grin against Mac's mouth, a touch of embarrassment creeping in. He sets me down, but doesn't let go. Christy comes over with her arms out, and only then does he release me so I can hug her. As soon as she lets go, his arm snakes back around my waist, drawing me close. Lucas walks toward us still holding his phone, flipping it around when he arrives. That's when I see he's been FaceTiming with the rest of the family in Steamboat Springs. Mac's parents, grandmother, and sister are squeezed into the frame. Susie's crying, and Nana is smiling like she has a secret. It makes me wonder if she suspected things early on. I wouldn't put it past her.

We wave and accept their congratulations.

"Hey, everyone," Darcy says. "Only two minutes until midnight. Who wants to dance into the new year with me?"

"Gotta go," Lucas says, hanging up on his family. Then he grabs Darcy's hand and they beeline back to the ballroom.

Christy gives Brooks a mischievous grin and drags him the same way.

"What do you think?" Mac asks.

I give a demure shrug, but my wide smile doesn't quite fit with the rest of my body language. "I wouldn't mind more time in your arms."

Mac's face breaks open into a radiant smile I've only seen a handful of times but hope to see often in the future. "I think we can make that happen, Sexy."

My eyebrows shoot up, surprised yet pleased by the sudden nickname. I reach up and pull his face down to give him a quick kiss, but he places his hands on my hips like he's settling in, and I certainly don't mind. It doesn't matter if we're dancing or kissing, as long as I'm doing it with the man I love.

The faint music coming from the ballroom turns into hundreds of voices chanting a countdown, but I hardly notice as we stay wrapped in one another's embrace, ringing in the new year in the best way possible.

Epilogue
Piper

One Year Later

The family is gathered in the Cahills' living room in anticipation of this year's White Elephant Exchange. We're waiting for Mac's uncle, who got stuck in traffic. I was looking forward to trying to make a snow dinosaur this year, but Lucas complained after the cookie decorating competition that I had an unfair advantage since I'm so creatively inclined and demanded we change it to something else. We had a team scavenger hunt instead, which was still lots of fun. And Elise and I pulled out the victory, which pretty much shut him up after that. He's just mad because his cookie didn't even place this year. Maybe he should have participated in the decorating class I conducted at Easter. It definitely helped Elise secure second place. Darcy swooped into third. She's surprisingly adept at icing cookies.

Darcy and Lucas have officially been dating for almost a year. I've heard rumors Nana has a ring to give him when he's ready. Lucas has improved his work-life balance. He still wants to kill it at work, but gives time with Darcy the priority she deserves, and I'm genuinely happy for them.

I gave my notice at work in January, having decided before the party that I wanted to give my painting career a chance. I had a nice cushion of savings that I'm using while I work on pieces for a gallery showing in Denver next month. Mac wants to keep them all for himself, but I promised him I'd paint something just for him once I'm finished with the show.

I've spent a lot of time traveling between Sumter, South Carolina, Denver, and Steamboat Springs this year. Mac's parents invited me and Maui to stay with them after I quit my job and, since Mac's career future was up in the air, I accepted. Christy lets me stay with her whenever I'm in Denver. I've loved sharing a house with Mac's parents, sister, and grandmother.

Elise has been super busy running the resort. She's got some new ideas to bring more visitors to the resort, and I think she'll make it even more successful than it already is. Though it sounds like there may be some hotshot long-time member giving her a little trouble. I'm sure she'll figure it out.

Susie and Hank have made good on their travel plans. Besides spending a month in Fiji, they toured Europe for several weeks this summer, and are making plans for an Alaskan cruise next year.

After more than a few conversations about our future, Mac decided he wanted to be closer to family, so he put in for a transfer to the Colorado Air National Guard in Aurora. He'll start there in the spring, which means we'll be moving back to the Denver area and closer to Christy, Lucas, and Darcy.

Even though we talked about a long engagement, we couldn't last even a full year and got married last month when everyone gathered together for Thanksgiving. I've temporarily moved to Shaw with Mac for his remaining few months, and his parents are graciously watching Maui for me here. I've already been house hunting in the Denver area, and we'll hop over there to check out a few houses after Christmas before flying back to South Carolina.

John finally arrives carrying a bag that most likely contains some sort of booze. I'm excited to see what everyone brought. This year I've classed it up a bit. The decoy box says my gift is a 10,000-piece puzzle of tiny, all-black pieces, but inside there's a puzzle of Steamboat Springs and a certificate for a trip for two to one of the hot springs in town. It exceeds the fifty-dollar limit, but I'm pretty sure the alcohol doled out last year did too. I can't wait to tell the recipient, though I already have an idea of who'll end up with it.

Susie hands out numbers. Lucas crows when he gets the coveted first pick. I can't wait to see what he thinks is the best gift. I have lucky number nine, which means I'm last, except for Lucas getting to go again. I'll keep that in mind when I make my selection.

After a very spirited forty minutes of opening and trading gifts, it's finally my turn. I pick up the only unopened gift bag left and then walk all the way around the circle, making a show of assessing all the gifts. John and Susie have bottles of wine. Elise is holding an *Elf*-themed mug with Christmas socks and a Starbucks gift card tucked inside. Hank unwrapped and kept a dozen golf balls. Darcy has a super soft sweater I'm pretty sure Elise brought. Lucas currently has a bottle of champagne, but he's eyeing the whiskey sampler in Nana's lap. And Mac is holding the puzzle I brought.

Right now, I'm leaning toward the *Elf* mug. Mac and I keep competing for the same Christmas mug each morning, and I wouldn't mind having a fun alternative on the days I don't make it to the kitchen first.

I sit down and reach into the gift bag, pulling out a heavy wad of tissue paper. Inside is a snow globe with a silver base. Inside the glass is a girl and a nutcracker standing in front of a Christmas tree. It reminds me of the painting Nana did last year. Is this her gift? The underside has a little crank. I turn it and "Dance of the Sugar Plum Fairy" plays. I clutch it to my chest, already imagining it sitting right next to the ice skaters.

"I love it," I say. "I'm not trading."

Lucas jumps up from his chair with his bottle of champagne.

"Then it's my turn. Nana, give me that whiskey."

He gives her the bottle and sits down. Elise groans.

"Guess that's it," she says.

"Now wait a minute," Nana says. "I haven't decided."

Elise perks up, wiggling her mug back and forth to show it off. Nana looks around the circle, pausing for an uncomfortably long moment on the snow globe in my hands. Then, she sits back in her seat.

"Never mind, I'll keep the bubbly."

I let out a relieved sigh, and Elise pouts for a second before taking the red, white, and green striped socks out of the mug and putting them on her feet. "At least I have coffee," she says cheerfully.

Mac leans over and points at my gift. "That comes with tickets to the ballet next year."

"What? I thought this was Nana's gift."

He smiles and shakes his head. "She brought the champagne."

I laugh. Of course, she did. I point at his box.

"Open that up. It's not as it seems."

He lets out a relieved sigh. "Oh, good. There's no way I'd have the patience for this."

He opens the box and peeks inside, pulling out a bag of puzzle pieces.

"So, a puzzle with no picture, then?"

I snicker. "I have the actual box for it, but keep looking. I wanted to make sure the actual gift was as disguised as possible."

He finds a small slip of paper and reads it before grinning over at me. "You little sneak! You knew no one else would want an all-black puzzle or bother to look inside the box."

I shrug. "So, who's going to be your plus one?"

"I think you know the answer to that," he says, surprising me with a bear hug that makes me squeal.

"Get a room, you two," Lucas says, but he's smiling.

I think he's truly happy for us. Of course, he's also in love, which doesn't hurt things. I don't think it'll be too long before Darcy has a ring on her finger, and I'll be just as excited for him.

I'll always be grateful to Lucas for bringing me here and introducing me to his family. If I'd never agreed to his crazy scheme, Mac and I would never have met, and I wouldn't have realized everything I was missing in my life. Lucas asked me once when it was I fell in love with his brother, and I told him. "It was while you were skiing."

I hope you enjoyed Piper and Mac's story.

Find additional content for the book, including a bonus epilogue, on my website at MeganByrd.net/wyws

Want to stay up-to-date on new book news? Sign up for my newsletter at MeganByrd.net/newsletter

Acknowledgments

Whew! Another book completed thanks to the help and support of many. I'm apt to forget a name or two, but know I greatly appreciate everyone who helped with this project in its various stages.

A huge thanks to Christy Brookshire, who's a Steamboat Springs expert and blessed me with pictures, brochures, and maps since I couldn't go in person. Thank you for answering my questions and reading an early draft to help ensure accuracy (all mistakes are mine, though I purposefully took a few liberties such as adding a grocer and liquor store to the downtown area). And thanks to her husband, Matt, for helping the skiing trails make better sense.

Thank you to Mike Whitten for talking with me about your time in the Navy on ships and navigating aircraft.

Thank you, Joe Biedenbach, for sharing your knowledge and experiences in the Air Force and answering my follow-up questions. I hope I did it justice.

Thank you, Sherri Wilson Johnson, author and Marco Polo extraordinaire, for letting me talk your ear off about all of my characters and ideas and providing feedback on my rambling thoughts, including the blasted blurb (my least favorite part). It's so fun to imagine and create with other writers!

Thank you to Anna and Cali, who gave feedback on the cover, among many other things. I cherish your friendship!

A big thank you to my Beta readers whose valuable input and time I do not take for granted: Heather, Lisa, Kelli, Sandy, Pattie, Hillary, Traci, Suzie, Jane, Regina, Keri, Tara, Mary Beth, Wenonah. Thank you also to my amazing ARC readers who spread the word online about my books.

Thank you to my immediate and extended family for your unwavering support throughout these years of writing and publishing.

And, of course, thank you, reader, for borrowing, buying, and/or hyping my book on social media and to your IRL friends. Your encouragement helps me continue on this journey of creating new stories for others to enjoy.

About the Author

Megan Byrd lives in Asheville, North Carolina with her husband and two kids. She hates running, but loves hiking in the mountains toward a waterfall or scenic view and taking kickboxing, HIIT, yoga, and Zumba classes. When she's not reading, writing, or chasing waterfalls, she enjoys visiting local bookstores, wandering through thrift shops in search of special gems, listening to live music, and catching up with friends.

Want to be first to know when the next book is available? Visit her website and sign up to receive e-newsletters which contain behind-the-scenes sneak peeks of her current work-in-progress, life updates, book recommendations, and other fun things. You'll also receive a free story (or two) for signing up! Follow her on social media for all the latest about current and upcoming novels.

Website: MeganByrd.net
Instagram: @megan.e.byrd
Facebook: AuthorMeganByrd